CHATEAUBRIAND
OR, TALES OF PERFORMANCE IN THE UNITED STATES

Matthew Lotti

ISBN-10: 0-9715594-5-7
ISBN-13: 978-0-9715594-5-5

For Joshua Collins

"The performance must take place at any cost, even if we have to do the impossible. Remember that this production is the thing on which your future depends."

- Konstantin Stanislavsky

1.

Marcel realized very quickly that it was ill-advised to stay up very late while in the Kensington State Behavioral Facility, since the disrupting sound blasts from the accompanying interns/patients snoring or groaning was loud enough to keep him awake, warm and frustrated - it was powerful enough to seep through the walls, to crawl through the pipes. It was something like two nights in that particular section of the Facility that brought him to rush under the covers so quickly and well before his 'bed time': the first night he wanted to stay up and scan the infomercials on television, the second he made a run for it at a much more reasonable hour, shuffling both slippers to his room, under the sheets and off into automated bliss. Being a naturally light sleeper, he needed all the advantages he could get. In bed, he kept the slippers on.

He spent most of his life being tossed around from school to school to youth center to behavioral facility to home to health facility and so on and so forth: strangers with glasses and pens kept asking him how he felt and they said something was wrong, and he kept agreeing with them because they looked so serious and what else should one think when met with poker faces and manila folders? *A life is a life in the barracks*! First outburst came at eight years of age, knocking down lunch trays, kicking in the legs of a cafeteria table, being dragged out of the room by the sleeve, wild swinging, lots of hushed astonishment. "Eat your food!" he screamed at his gawking peers, though they kept looking.

1. His parents were both 25 when he was conceived.

2. He was born average weight and average height.
3. He was born with no defects or food allergies.
4. His parents lived in a middle-to-upper income neighborhood just outside of Philadelphia.
5. An early intelligence test that he took when he was six or seven years old showed he had a slightly above average IQ.

The school psychologist, a bachelor without a bobby-soxer but with a tweed jacket, made Marcel talk and talk, and while Marcel talked he listened, but what the school psychologist heard wasn't satisfactory, so Marcel talked more and more, and though he couldn't remember the line of questioning, he always remembered connecting words together on the Magnetic WordBoard, like "hand head" and "class self," that was set up by the school psychologist for him to play with. Parents were summoned, the teacher was summoned, and then his parents and the teacher were summoned together. He was made nervous by the attention, and though he apologized repeatedly for his transgression it wasn't enough to call off the hunt. Outbursts were never dismissed.

It was arranged for him to meet a woman doctor after school who asked Marcel more questions. Marcel was asked if he liked school, and he said yes. He was asked if he liked his classmates, and he said yes. He was asked if his parents were fighting, and he said no, not at all. She wanted him to tell her about what led to the yelling and anger-discharge, and every time he said something - anything - she always probed for more details. She wanted an exact verbal description, from Marcel's subjective viewpoint of the event. Marcel couldn't do it, but she insisted. Marcel decided to start embellishing. For every meeting they had - every week, every Wednesday - he had to explain class work assignments, whether or not he felt he was being treated fairly, whether he was having trouble understanding mathematics. Eventually, he took pleasure in the telling of the story - from the beginning - and going forward, marching proudly. He'd introduce new individuals to the woman by talking about their hair or their clothing, some odd trait they had that he noticed, how he felt about them, what they said to him throughout the week. In fact, some of his imitations of them and their tics made her laugh, and that kind of response encouraged him to take things to their comedic limit, eventually going overboard. Trained in this, the woman doctor challenged him on the fantastic steps from reality, forcing him to explain and explain clearly, but being mindful not to cause her to lose her belief in the story or lose her attention. The unnerving outbursts in school didn't stop, but Marcel's observational skills were greatly improved. He was learning about communication.

Yet the ability to communicate to this woman did not translate to school, where he encountered problem after problem with faculty and students over a series of incidents and eventual shouting matches. Marcel would refuse to back down from them or anyone else, and on one occasion he had to be physically restrained by the speech teacher who saw him feverishly bolt down the hallway after a blond-headed student who Marcel thought moved his coat off the coat rack and throw it onto the floor. Had the speech teacher not intervened, the blonde-headed boy would have been struck by the closed-fisted attack.

At home, Marcel was much more comfortable and relaxed, comforted by the sanctity of his room and the stable atmosphere around him. His younger Sister Lucile did her best to avoid him - she was more frightened by him than her parents thought - and since the two of them had separate rooms, territory was never an issue. He was prone to fits, but his Mother was able to sit and talk to him - she was a trained learning specialist (she did not work in the same school district she placed Marcel and Lucile in for fear of seeming like a Meddling Mother). The psychiatrists and other Medical Types she consulted suggested home schooling, but she didn't have the desire to stay at home and regulate his learning and she felt the lack of social contact was inherently unhealthy and counterproductive. She conferred with her husband and he had the same outlook. He couldn't take time off from work, since he had a seafood company to run and more than a dozen employees to closely monitor.

As medical intervention, Pill Type A was prescribed at 7 - with the dosage increased a few years later - but he was still significantly jittery, fond of scaling objects and moving about endlessly. When he developed severe headaches the dosage was lowered, but then it became almost completely ineffective and his (then) doctor decided to experiment with several doses of different prescriptions taken on alternating days - but that caused stomach cramps and then diarrhea on a weekly basis (Friday would be the day, like clockwork, he would get sick, at around 4 PM, right after school). Another pill they tried made him flushed and sweaty. Blood work was taken, tests were run, sessions were conducted with the different psychiatrists he was then switched to - the previous one was considered "not helpful" in the conversation Marcel's Mother would have with the new one and the new one would always nod slightly but refrain from verbal agreement.

Despite the medicine and counseling he was bumped out of five schools in a span of six years, constantly moving from location to location, chair to chair, room to room; the teachers and homerooms he was placed in were armed - before he set foot in the room - with summary reports and testing results, teachers fully aware of their new student's past history and prejudiced because of it. None of the new teachers were ready to accept the challenge, figuring he would be a lost cause and a room distraction. Marcel's Mother would meet with them and sympathize with their intolerance, and the teachers - some hardened veterans, some 23-year-old fawns - would smatter her with advice and recommendations and she would nod approvingly but shrug dismissively. They would unfurl their evidence incident by incident, citing cases where Marcel did this or that, where he grabbed the table and attempted to overturn it and the numerous books on top, the time he grabbed the class hamster and chucked it into the hallway, crushing it, the Tourette-like shouting during class, the back-talk. And Marcel's Mother would listen.

He was placed in the Pennsylvania Youth Correction Center and Assisting Facility (hereafter "PYCCAF") at fourteen when it became clear no one else could help him - his violence had only increased and he was taken to demolishing things in his own room, occasionally injuring himself and then being mad at himself for accidentally injuring himself. At PYCCAF, he encountered some people better off than him and some worse, like Trevor, who would often strip in the middle of the room for attention. He and Trevor became an ungodly alliance, with Trevor influencing Marcel to become creative. Marcel would often point out to Trevor who was, as he termed it, "The Bitch of the Day," a person picked at random, who would be the target of harassment and criticism. Some of the other youth patients grew tired and scared of this, so they formed their own alliance and retaliated by throwing chairs and shouting; staff had to ultimately separate the two to try and keep peace. Marcel received his elementary and secondary education at PYCCAF, after having been unable to stay anywhere else for an extended period of time.

Outside of PYCCAF, Marcel had few close friends. One day in the summer he was standing, for no real reason, in the doorway of his home, looking around his neighborhood. He saw two girls down the street that were playing basketball. He impulsively opened the door, walked over and asked if he could join in, that he had nothing to do, that he would play fair. The two girls looked at each other suspiciously and the one with pigtails said no, sorry, him joining would make it unfair - 2 against 1. So he volunteered to play against the two of them. The girls found this more acceptable and started off a new game. Their talent and accuracy were far better than his - he had only played basketball in gym class a few times prior - and his defense was non-existent. The girls insisted he let them win, to which he shrugged and laughed, and promptly thanked them and ran back to his home, relieved.

A few days later the two girls appeared at his front door and asked if he wanted to play again. Having nothing to do, once more - Marcel quickly finished his meager homework and went outside with them. Marcel's Mother, home on vacation, would check outside to ensure everyone's safety, but Marcel got along well with the girls. He even found out their names: Amelia and Regine. Marcel wasn't comfortable talking to the two of them at the beginning, but settled in eventually. Amelia's Mother - whose house they played at - would also keep a watchful eye on the three of them, and in time, both Marcel's Mother and Amelia's Mother met, became friends, and had lunch with each other at least once a week. Amelia's Mother was an avid painter - it was her hobby - and it was through her encouragement that Marcel's Mother began doing some basic landscapes and barns and very loose imitations of Monet. Marcel's Father would complement her and hang them up in his office. Marcel's Father thought that painting would be good for his wife's stress and nerves; he preferred yoga and meditation.

It was the decision of one of Marcel's doctors about two years later - Doctor #14, by his count - that he should try to attend high school, since the medication was apparently working - Marcel's 'breakdowns' were minimized and he had been communicative and verbally open with him, answering his questions, being honest (Q: "What did you think about going to all those different schools? Did it make you scared?" A: "At first, but then I thought it was interesting to see so many different places whereas someone else might go to school with the same people for years and years.") and following directions given to him. Doctor #14 explained to Marcel's parents that keeping Marcel in PYCCAF and away from high school was detrimental to him, that reintegration would be the best route to take next. Marcel's parents decided to place him in Borleau Academy, which would be the school Amelia and Regine were attending, and they might be a source of support.

Marcel met with his assigned 55-year-old counselor twice a day. This one never asked Marcel any personal questions, never requested that Marcel speak of his day or describe his friends and associates to him - while he sat in the counselor's office, the counselor made him fill out some questionnaires while he scribbled in notepads, checked boxes on forms and made phone calls, usually about other students or to people Marcel did not know. He did not particularly like this counselor, but refrained from saying so to his parents. The only thing Marcel was asked - if they met in the hallways while classes were changing - was if Marcel took his medication for the day. It did not seem to be the time or place to be asked such a thing, so Marcel would nod and remember to try to avoid him in the future.

At lunchtime, he ran into the problem of finding a place to sit. This was stressful, and even though he would spot Amelia at one of the tables - who, if she saw him, would wave him over - he politely declined and sat in the corner with one or two other people usually immersed in a book of sorts or doing something they didn't want interrupted by lunchtime chatter. He met and sparked up conversation with Josef, a sophomore who spent his time constructively, making doodles and cartoons in an 8 x 10 notebook while picking into a bag of carrots and celery that was his lunch. Josef showed Marcel one of what he called his "side projects," a comic strip based on some of his friends from school that didn't have his same lunch period that were done in a cartoony/caricaturized way. He refrained from drawing teachers and stuck to students only ("for ethical reasons"). He tried to keep the strip about people he knew and liked and could take the joke. It was creative, considering the limitations he placed on the strip and the timeframe he made it in (one 45 minute period; the rest of his day was booked): he would put his characters in various real-life situations that were in the newspaper he had tucked into his backpack, and parody the news - like making one particular student with a rigid gait a Senator who was always doing some sort-of spin control to deflect criticism; he had another friend talking (inexplicably) to a small toy monkey to take a jab at this particular peer's flighty nature. Some students that heard about or saw the drawings (he didn't hand them out to everyone for fear of making enemies, but his friends did sometimes pass them out, against his explicit instructions) gave him money or tickets to movies or art supplies in exchange for full-page caricatures of them to put in their bedrooms or lockers - he found their interest in his work to be uplifting but also didn't want to be pressured to work on something he didn't feel naturally inclined to make.

Since he began talking to Josef (and Josef warmed up to him), Marcel no longer feared lunch, but still dreaded Biology, because two students in there - Gary and Gary's friend Chris (who he sat next to) - just started harassing him during the entire class for no real reason - in the same way there was no real definable reason why some people couldn't get along together or judge each other by appearance alone ("I don't like him - I don't like the way he looks at me"). For Biology class, Marcel was the Omega, and Gary was the Alpha. (It wouldn't be until three years later that Marcel would realize why he became the target: Marcel's assigned lab partner was Kirsten Glotzer, who

Gary was secretly pining for - his brutality would be his attempt to make himself look good at weak Marcel's expense and eventually win her over; remarkably, Kirsten fell for it, Marcel was told later, and the two of them became an item.) Every day in class Gary and Chris would cook up ways to harass or insult or hurt him: they kicked him under the table, jabbed him with a compass, squirted him with a miniature squirt gun, all when the teacher - a dumbtwat woman named Mrs. Nisseri who was difficult to understand because of her atrocious accent (no one was sure what country she came from, but she must have learned English late - as stated in linguistics: the older you are, the less capable you are of being 'fluent' in a language) - turned around, and even when she looked at the class, she was mostly oblivious to things going on.

What made it worse was that he didn't know anyone at this Private School that well (except for Amelia and Regine), and by the time he arrived, alliances had already been formed by the students, who had all known each other from past years together. Because of these cliques and groups and such, and because of his outsider status, he was easy to target. The other kids in the class who were behind Gary and Chris would watch Marcel get teased with rapt amusement, and pitifully, most of those who found it hilarious were female. None rushed to his side, no one told Gary or Chris to leave him alone. Even Kirsten, who sat to the right of Marcel, would say, "Hey Gary, you know what Marcel said about you?" and make up some lie to stir the proverbial pot. The entire class enjoyed the display and looked forward to it: obnoxiously, one female walking in class behind Marcel was overheard saying to another girl, "I was supposed to meet Mr. Allman [the band instructor] at this time but rescheduled it for the next period." The girlfriend asked why. "I can't miss this class. It's a riot." Marcel turned his head at both of them and they sneered.

Marcel managed to keep himself under control for several months, keeping quiet on the incidents in class. He kept it from his parents, counselors and doctors. He discussed the issue with Amelia, after school, to see what he should do.

AMELIA: Tell your mom. Or Mrs. Nisseri. That has to stop.

MARCEL: Mrs. Nisseri won't listen.

AMELIA: You have to do something or tell somebody.

MARCEL: I don't want to bother anyone.

AMELIA: Gary's an asshole and Chris is a bigger asshole for following him. They shouldn't get away with that. Just tell her to move your seat.

… which Marcel did. So Mrs. Nisseri moved Marcel's seat to a different location, only to have Gary and Chris switch seats with the two new kids Marcel was placed next to the minute the classroom phone rang (which it did, a lot) and Nisseri stepped out into the hallway to take it. Everyone in class was watching and laughing and talking out loud - they were the chorus for this minor play. When Marcel turned to look at the two, they smiled at him. This move proved to be the End Point, as an enraged Marcel stood up, put his shoe on top of the stool like he was going to tie it, grabbed the stool from under his foot and began swinging violently at Chris (who was closer), bringing the stool down on his defending arm and continuing to swing at his body and legs (Chris fell to the floor and tried to use his own stool to block). Gary, seeing this, stood and backed up towards the window to avoid getting hit; the screaming from the girls in class was enough to bring Nisseri back in the room. She yelled in the hallway for a Hall Monitor to come quickly, and the Hall Monitor was the one who came in to restrain Marcel; reinforcements from down the hall appeared and intervened. It took, in all, four people - including Marcel's counselor, who came in last - to hold him down. The experience of having grown adults leaning on him and pinning his arms was not unfamiliar to him. He tried to turn his head to see if he hurt either Gary or Chris, but someone's palm was covering his left eye.

This relapse was enough to put Marcel back into PYCCAF, but now PYCCAF was saying to Marcel's strung-out parents that they recommend he be put into the Juvenile Wing of Kensington State Behavioral Facility, where he'd be in a more 'controlled' environment. That was the word they used, 'controlled.' It was determined that Marcel would, while living there, continue his studies and receive support and therapy. In two years, he would be transferred from the Juvenile Wing to the Adult Wing, which the staff told Marcel's parents in the beginning wouldn't happen - that he'd spend (at most) six months there and no more - but it did.

2.

In terms of passions or interests, Marcel had several - none major - and could be absorbed by multiple subjects, fields and interests. When he was younger, he was fascinated by rare coins (sparked by a considerable collection bestowed upon him by his Grandmother) and the family's first computer, an Apple IIc, on which he played a game called "Math Blaster" which helped his arithmetic skills considerably - he also learned the basics of typing using a very primitive program that came free with the system. When he got older, it became baseball - he collected the cards and put them in a book (but never set foot on a baseball diamond and never cared to play - only watch the games on television) and swimming. Older still, he found interest in the deceptive simplicity of basketball (inspired by Amelia and Regine) and liked to scan through books on travel (which he took out from the library using his Dad's account). Eventually, everything was fascinating: magazines of every type that could hold his focus: from photography to sculpture to music to theater. It clicked in his head while in his reading class at Kensington State: the class was reading *The Most Dangerous Game*, and one of the kids in his class said it was boring. The teacher asked him why he thought it was boring. He said it just was. The teacher asked to explain why. The boy couldn't. Then the teacher said: If something is boring after two minutes, try it for four. If still boring, then eight. Then sixteen. Then thirty-two. Eventually, you should realize that it is not boring at all. It must be made interesting. People are interesting, things are interesting, places are interesting, information is interesting. The boy the teacher was speaking to didn't understand or care to understand, but Marcel processed the message.

When Marcel was 19, he became interested in Daphne, and with the interest in Daphne came the interest in self-pleasure. From 15-18 he was mostly a 'dabbler,' taking time in the corner of his room or under his covers to dream and create only about once a week - it wasn't a steady action. Daphne was the Eve that created consistency and caused the habit to stick, and the time in the corner of the room or the time under the covers wasn't enough. She was an intern from one of the local colleges who was helping out the staff at Kensington, who wanted to work in a situation like that when she got out of school. Her every task was meted out by the Head Nurse, a dour and uncivilized mass whose own bipolarity made her placement in the realm of authority to be a gag too ludicrous not to be true. The Head Nurse looked like she wanted to handle the unpleasantries of the job herself; young nurse Daphne was buoyant and wispy and worked hard to appear calm.

Marcel realized the disgusting quality of such a job because of his own situation and his ability to look around him and ask questions - he was surrounded by formless, pear-shaped men with slumped shoulders and wild faces and of wavering opinion, and every interaction was a potential altercation. It was not in Marcel's advantage to act like them or be either overly exuberant or disturbingly reclusive for fear of scaring her away from him. He didn't want to embarrass himself or bring extensive attention to himself, and, when she was around, tried to be discreet in behavior, only speaking to her or looking directly at her if need be, and even being extra polite to the Head Nurse, who was most often right around the corner.

… But his ignoring her was self-defeating and frustrating: why ignore when you can lavish with attention? So he tested his luck one day - a day he planned well ahead of time. When sitting in his room he would politely look her in the eye and recite his pre-formulated inquiry. He didn't want to improvise at the last minute out of concern that he might say something that could potentially be interpreted in any way but what was intended (he would have written it down had he not had his box of charcoals and watercolors removed from his room by the staff as punishment for getting some residue on the sheets of his bed). As she came in to check on the room's condition alone - the Head Nurse, after two months, allowed Daphne to handle some primary functions on her own - Marcel smiled warmly and said:

MARCEL: Miss, I'm sorry. I've been meaning to ask you a question. Do you mind?

DAPHNE: What would that be?

MARCEL: Why do you want to be here?

It was a legitimate question, he thought, and self-depreciating as well. His early plan was to be smooth and 'knowing,' but he voted down the Martini Vibe since he's never had a martini and couldn't trust what he saw on television. He thought, after that bunk initial idea, to just attack the complexity of the situation by showing her that he could think clearly, that he could be conversive, that he was trained to speak his mind in a rational manner, that he could explain situations, scenes, relay complex anecdotes. He was also curious as to why she would want such a job - what led her to her career choice.

DAPHNE: Why do I want to be in this room?

MARCEL: Why you want to be in this building, why you'd want the job you have.

DAPHNE: (*Pause*) I think, well, I think it's because it always interested me.

MARCEL: The mind?

DAPHNE: Helping those that need my help.

MARCEL: Were you ever a candy striper?

DAPHNE: I did some volunteer work for the Red Cross when they had their Teen Program set up. I'm still new to this, but it's interesting.

MARCEL: (*Nodding*) Do you like it now? In here?

DAPHNE: I'm still learning a lot. There's a lot to learn. But it's *interesting*, I suppose. (*Pause*) If you need anything else, please let one of us know.

At this, she began her retreat from the room, maintaining minimal eye contact while steadily moving backwards. Marcel returned to the book his was reading before she entered, confident that his first attempt at throwaway dialogue with her went as well as could be expected at this time. He felt he would get better with age.

He then intended to completely ignore her - to not ask any more questions, not interrogate, don't even bother. He didn't want to make her think he was after her in any way. Some of the other patients started getting forward, asking her to dance when one of the patients had a small birthday party. They put music on and tried to make conversation with her - Marcel personally sought the offenders later and admonished them for bothering the staff, concocting some lie that the Head Nurse wasn't happy with them for being so rude. Most of the time his fellow travelers were grateful that Marcel told them about it and next time used more caution. Marcel's scare tactics worked.

The number of people he had to converse with was small, however, so in-between meetings with doctors and nurses and casual visits from his parents (and, rarely, a visit from Amelia and Regine, who brought him presents around the holidays and he felt ashamed they had to see him in his paleness), he managed to befriend the Maintenance Crew. He found them to be the most outrageous and extroverted and personable of the staff, and they were usually first to initiate contact with him, asking him non-personal questions about this, or that, if he saw the football game on television or whatnot. They tried to talk to all of the patients - Marcel thought it was a part of their 'joke,' to chat with the crazies - and he was one of the only ones who bothered to respond. One of them that he always saw, a big burly man who wore the same red cap, was interested in cars, and though Marcel liked cars but didn't know a lot about them, this man would talk on and on about them, and Marcel would listen and ask questions about this and that - generic ones, like what was the fastest and what was the most expensive, and the maintenance man always had some sort of answer. Marcel didn't care all that much, but the man's passion made him pay attention.

Instead of talking, which he didn't have to do, Marcel resorted to watching hours and hours of television, which was almost always on and almost everyone was intrigued by and which the pamphlet said would be on only certain hours of the day but was only off about six hours throughout the entire day. There was no program as to what would be on - the nurses decided - so whatever they randomly clicked on was what everyone would watch. The brunette reporter woman that did her daily spiel live from Wall Street caught Marcel's eye, and he made a point to watch her every week day, at 11:20 in the morning, which was when she was on discussing highs and lows. She could have been talking about carrots or hand grenades, but her mouth was a dazzling light show, bending and flexing waves of sound and calm. She was delicate and knowledgeable. The weather woman on the local news at 5:45 wore an earth-toned business suit every night and had a very rigid posture which, to Marcel, represented power and force, while her consistently perfect amber hair and pixie visage suggested delicacy - a wonderful balance. He enjoyed watching her as well.

Other than television times, Marcel spent most of the day displeased with the schedule made up for him by the staff, which placed him in activities he didn't feel were necessary, like Chess Club, the Board Games Club and

Swimming (which he had, by that time, become tired of). He brought up his problems with the Head Doctor.

MARCEL: I don't care for any of those. There's nothing wrong with them, I would just rather do some other things.

DOCTOR: You're supposed to present your complaints to one of the schedule coordinators.

MARCEL: They don't listen.

DOCTOR: Do you want me to talk to them?

MARCEL: Yes. If you could.

The Head Doctor asked him what he wanted to participate in, and the Doctor did her part to ask the coordinators to meet with Marcel and ask him what he wanted to do. He stayed in the Book Club and the Yoga Class (which Marcel's Father was delighted to hear he tried), and begged them to let him have one 45-minute period each day - instead of swimming - where he could practice shooting hoops in the gymnasium, just by himself, and he made up some reason why that wouldn't be a problem. Not wanting to hear from the Head Doctor again, the schedule coordinators let him have his way, and each day he put on his sweatpants and t-shirt and practiced his dribbling and free throws. (He also tried to organize a Drama Club after reading the biographical entry for the Marquis de Sade in the yellowing encyclopedia that was in the library and finding the idea to be clever, but no one would hear it.)

Physically, or more properly, internally, he was being consumed and dismantled by the different medications he was taking, Pills Yellow and Blue - every Friday, like clockwork, he suffered with diarrhea, but unlike before, it would go on Saturday and Sunday as well. It started off as cramping, then pain, then a gradual procession to and from the bathroom resumed. He told the nurses and doctors about it, so they gave him Gatorade, claiming it replenished lost electrolytes, and they made him eat nothing but bananas and cottage cheese and yogurt. Just as long as he didn't start suffering from nausea or vomiting or tachycardia, they told him, he'd be all right.

In terms of sexual functioning, the medication had no effect. An older man - roughly Marcel's Uncle's age (late 50's) - gave him a sermon on how his 'piping' was not working the way it should and the causes. This man, whose name Marcel chose not to remember because he did not like his presence (the man took issue with everything - the food was cold, or the cushions to the couch were dirty - but smelled foul himself, of bestial sweating and staleness), barked about how he was fine before they gave him what he called "those red bastards" which he said ruined any drive or ambition. "I don't like not having my spurs on," he said, "and I'm still young, too." Before this man's breakdown, Marcel was told, he was active and vibrant, and even kept a mistress who he would meet in a designated bar at a designated time, have a couple of drinks and scurry out to a motel where they would do their business and talk about their families. The man's midnight friend was raising three children, had just enough customers to allow her to pay for new shoes, clothes and food. One of her clients - not this man Marcel was sitting with - bought her a Lexus for Christmas. When Marcel asked for details about the Lexus - so he could talk to the car freak from maintenance about it later - the man cut him off, and said that was all he knew, and that he didn't care about the car. The man confessed that when he thought about her when he was jerking off in the bathroom, it was just sweat spaghetti. It bothered him, but in another way, it eliminated the constant urge, and kicked him out of the hunt. Marcel didn't ask what caused the man to be in the same room he was, or if he liked it there - he learned his lesson asking that kind of question, more or less, with Daphne. That was one of the many men he listened to. He was too young for them to listen to him.

Most of his time outside of supervision, since they were spent in relative peace and quiet, involved fantasizing. By fantasizing, Marcel's hopes and passions were inflamed and relentless - he was deprived of the social settings and diversity a regular individual was exposed to. His thoughts culled up imaginary worlds with girls he barely knew, those he saw and maybe exchanged a few words with: the redhead with glasses who was defiantly thin, the long-haired brunette with the acid-tongue and perpetual scowl whose Father was a surgeon and whose Mother was a teacher, Kirsten, his Female Judas, for betraying him in Biology Class, taking pleasure in the abuse - she had a baby face and athletic build, she played basketball and smoked Lucky Strikes in the cemetery outside of school. While sitting next to her, he could smell the caustic perfume linger around her skin, and remember how she would brush her hair or adjust her makeup. He had a fantasy queue, a finite listing of potential scenarios and events that involved the aforementioned girls, brief glimpses of whom he saw in commercials or interviewed on the news, and manipulated them in an assortment of situations and predicaments that he would assign. They weren't rape fantasies straight out of Asian Cinema, but the mental stories and constructs tended to get teasingly rough and consensually deviant. The girls were interchangeable - one body simply became a substitute for another, they were all the same to him - and the molecular structure of his fantasy was flexible as well. For instance, one fantasy had him on the bus getting driven back home, and across the aisle from him would be one of the girls - though usually Annette, the sassy brunette, since she actually sat there on their bus rides home - and she would be facing him, and he facing her, and the game they would play was: the emptier the bus got, the more clothes they would remove, starting with simple unbuttoning and moving towards wholesale disrobing and, ultimately, watching each other finger themselves. Another had

Marcel and one female in the school showers washing each other and then getting somewhat rough, lightly smacking each other on the side or arm and then chasing each other into the locker area where, wet and red, they would tussle on the cold floor.

But the problem with fantasies - with Marcel, at least - was that the girls in his mind were outdated concepts or pure visual conjuring: they were girls from his past, mostly from his past, girls he didn't become friends with, or intimate with on any emotional level, so with passing time it became tiresome to pleasure himself to the idea of them, when those ideas became antiquated and logically unreasonable. The distance in space and time between him and them was growing: they were intangible, almost nonexistent. The endgame was to keep updating the butterfly boxes, to keep the variety rolling. The floor he lived on was predominately male; the images of the unreachable women on the television were insufficient, the thought of Amelia and Regine was too familiar (almost taboo), so therefore Daphne became his animated object of desire. It was highly unlikely that Marcel and her could ever have a future together in any way, but it wasn't impossible: he saw her and she saw him and, like a Father once told his son, "Men always fall in love with their nurses," and this went for Papa Hemingway, currently himself and certainly others in the past and future.

He would imagine her dressing - putting on her long white coat and loose-fitting pants, he would try to guesstimate her dress size, the size of her brassiere, whether or not she wore panties or boxers (some did, he heard), how often she washed her face, whether she enjoyed the smell of stale, febrile men so much to immerse herself in them, whether she'd ever been touched, whether she had a boyfriend and all the particulars: the day routine scheduled and carried out - not to mention the primitive token economy in place to establish models for good behavior and Special Incentives and Privileges - and the absence of people to speak and listen to or learn from left him needing things to occupy his time, and that time filler became her. Her in his wants all day long, washing him, talking to him, telling him about herself. If she could be handed the dailies of his celluloid creations and what she'd be directed to do, she'd have been horrified. So he kept everything a secret. And no one paid attention.

Marcel pleasured himself while eating, while sitting, while in a group meeting, when he first woke up: he became awesomely skilled - out of necessity - of hiding his tracks and minimalist movement. The semen would flow down his pant leg; he'd dismiss himself to the rest room, wipe up. If he were in a situation where he couldn't move, he'd focus in on the sensation of the wetness running down his left calf, wondering how much of it got past his ankles and into his slippers. He didn't even have to move much or even use his hands - he'd position himself so the erect head was sticking out of his underpants, and squirm around so that the elastic band rubbed on the top and his leg rubbed the bottom, and after a little while of doing that, accompanied by delirious fantasy, it would release. Other times, when in bed, he would position himself face down on the mattress and rotate his lower torso in circles, rubbing the top of his penis against his underwear and the soft mattress. When time and solitude was provided, the ordinary hand-on approach worked.

Others were not always so cautious, and were spotted by the staff and harshly reprimanded; one red-headed man on the same floor was a repeat offender: he would stare at various objects around the room and satisfy himself, pants around the ankles, standing or sitting. Marcel would see him doing it while playing Solitaire, or just in the middle of the corridor, and this sight was more comical than ominous to him, and even the staff thought it was a ghoulish but very amusing running joke: the red-headed man wasn't ominous or predatory, he was merely adrift. When it became a severe epidemic, though, the joke had to end, and the orderlies were told to take him to another wing, in another setting, and when he came back he appeared different: he no longer stared, but shook, and was never found performing such acts again. Marcel couldn't ask him what happened, since the man hardly spoke, and even thought about inquiring with the staff, although he knew they weren't permitted to tell him. Was he given the same red pills the man with the prostitute friend had?

Knowing that the Hawks were keeping a close eye on the ward and any gyrations or perverse gestations could be spotted, Marcel was forced to operate swiftly, silently and with a degree of stealth. Letting Daphne, only a few feet away, see him would be disastrous: his examination of her had to be discreet, and his eyes had to move from her body and back to the television or his magazine naturally.

One of the digressions he was tempted to pull off was taking one of the nurses uniforms - they kept some clean, unused ones in the closet that had a broken lock or was never locked in the first place - and trying it on. The thought of doing it was unexplainable - Marcel had no rational reason except for pure thrills - so it was essentially a matter of nonsensical fetishism. On the plus side, if *he* was caught he would know what happened to the red-haired man.

The day he was going to try for it was planned out ahead of time, like his planned conversation with Daphne was ... but he hoped this attempt would be more successful in execution. It was meticulously staked out, planned (he peeked inside the closet door while walking by and got an idea where the uniforms were kept); the diversion of planning the clothing siege was a pleasant relief from the devastating boredom of going to meetings, being counseled, and shooting hoops alone. The hallways were usually abandoned, contrary to popular opinion that a "madhouse" was frenzied and frenetic, and the overseeing eyes thought to prowl the hallways at night was just a myth of the patients' creation - truth be told, few people were around (some security aside), the lights were out, there were no security cameras, the doors were not locked. Marcel kept watch, and frequently turned around to survey the hallway behind him, but nothing and no one was there.

When opening the closet door, he used supreme delicacy, turning to the left as slowly as his hand could move, and then pulling with his entire upper body. Once open, he stepped inside but kept his one slipper wedged in the door to allow enough glow from the emergency lights in the hallway to shine into the closet. He fumbled around a little, but remembered from his staking out what part of the room they were haphazardly tossed in boxes. Why they were in the boxes or in this particular closet didn't make sense - Marcel thought the nurses received their clothing from a company outside the facility - but the fact was that they were there and he had found them. Without spending extensive time reaching for the correct size, he swiped the first pair of pants and top he could find (he had to hold them to the light coming in from the door to make sure they were at least close to what he wanted), he removed his slipper and shut the door.

With his new prize, he scampered over to the men's bathroom, hid in the back stall and tried it on. The outfit was entirely too small for him - it clung to his flesh and squeezed every inch it was covering. With the pants ¾ of the way on, and the fresh top buttoned snuggly, he started to jerk off with a palm full of water and some soap from the sink. The smell from the closet was still in the clothes - it commingled with the bathroom air. But Marcel could not be fazed. He would break for fifteen minutes in-between sessions to make sure his semen was wiped off the bathroom walls and sink rims - he used the sleeve from the top so he didn't have to bother with paper towels. The time spent in the bathroom was unknown, but by the time his penis was bleeding from accidentally scratching it with the corner of his thumbnail, he realized it was time to stop and try to get sleep.

Not sure what to do with the uniform, which was soiled and moist with his sweat, he took the top of the garbage can lid off, emptied the paper towels on the floor, and threw in the uniform top and bottom. He contemplated returning it, but was too tired to bother. If he got caught, he thought, it was for the best. *You can only take, you can't give.*

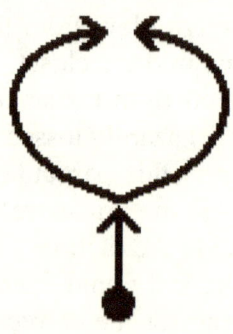

3.

Marcel was discharged from the Kensington State Behavioral Facility three months after the clothing incident, and permanently separated from Daphne, whom he knew he would miss and think about. The clothes were found by the janitorial crew, and reported to the nurses and staff, who held a meeting with all of the patients on the floor, immediately suspecting the red-haired man and dealing with him individually. Marcel didn't know what happened to the man - he was taken away for a period of time and returned shortly thereafter - but felt bad that his digression caused problems for him. It was not Marcel's intent to implicate anyone else in his plan; it simply happened that way.

The doctors and staff felt that with the right medication working for him, Marcel could return home and that his behavior was 'leveled out,' that what they told his parents should have happened a long time ago eventually came to pass - that simply aging was beneficial to him and aided his recovery. He was still to be monitored and have regular appointments with his family physician and see his therapist once a week, for however long a session the therapist felt was needed. His parents were pleased to have him home, and he was pleased to be returning to them. He was out of his teens, and it was time he occupied himself in a more suitable and productive fashion. Above all, Marcel was going to miss his own gymnasium.

He had asked the Doctor what he could do or should do, and the Doctor placed the responsibility on his parents, who were assigned the task of monitoring and guiding, instead of waving to him across the table and letting him run free. The first few days at home, back in his real room - a strangely foreign and untouched den that required instant rearranging and repainting - he could do nothing but cry and apologize - apologize to his parents for putting him through it all, to his Sister for (no doubt) suffering the slings and arrows, for the stigma his existence imposed, and they all said they understood and hugged him and promised to be cooperative. It was a period of adjustment - he could be fine, he felt fine.

His parents got used to his presence very quickly, dished out his meals, discussed T(errible) V(audeville) shows and current events - which Marcel was staying up-to-date with them on, considering the fact that he read the newspaper every day at Kensington and no one else would - and everyone tried to get to know one another again. Lucile, on the other hand, saw him as a foreign entity, a space oddity, as if someone invited a stranger to live with her and watch her eat and share and exchange air - she did not adjust so easily. Marcel took up her visible coldness with his Mother, who tried to portray Lucile's side fairly.

MOTHER: You have to understand it's strange for your Sister to get used to you. And, well, I guess she's a little scared. And maybe angry. But she's 16 - she's scared and angry about her skin in the morning and always complaining about people in her class.

MARCEL: It's strange for me, too.

MOTHER: I know it is.

MARCEL: And you. And Dad.

MOTHER: We're managing.

MARCEL: Can you talk to her for me, then? She's making me feel guilty about being back home.

MOTHER: I already did. She promised me she'd try. She has a lot on her mind. She's in that awkward stage.

MARCEL: I'm in my awkward stage, too.

MOTHER: No, you're past that.

Despite this parental intervention, Marcel and Lucile argued about almost everything. Several times Marcel was so taken with her inconsiderate behavior he was tempted to hit her, so he would flee the room and try to stay away from her. He knew she hated it when he answered the phone - he tended to converse with the same person on the other line for an extended period of time, sometimes getting to know them well, knowing how they know Lucile - so he tried not to answer it. Likewise, she hated how their Father had to divide his time between the two of them to teach them both how to drive (she wanted all the attention). To compensate, Father taught Marcel and Mother taught Lucile. They took the test the same day, one after the other (Marcel let her go first because she wanted to and he was too nervous). After the test, and they both passed, they went out for a celebratory dinner, during which Lucile tried to kill Marcel's spirit by asking whether or not it was 'safe' for him to be driving. Marcel glared at her, and their Father told them to stop it. Their Mother saw the bickering as quaint, standard rivalry, and healthy, and only intervened when things became so loud she feared *others would hear*.

While he was settling back in his childhood home, Marcel met with and spent time talking to Amelia whenever she was around about what happened in each other's lives - she was attending Bryn Mawr (and living on campus), double majoring in acting and sociology, and had gotten into some small-scale painting like her Mother (and Marcel's Mother). The two had a lot to discuss and catch up on, and the conversation flowed smoothly - she had a boyfriend she was seeing, however neither developed seriously romantic inclinations towards each other and she almost preferred not to mention him at all. Marcel and Amelia, on clear days when Amelia was home and had time, would play one-on-one outside … and to her surprise,

Marcel had remarkably improved his game, beating her twice in a row. She was shocked by his sudden proficiency.

MARCEL: It was almost all I did while at the center. Rarely - if ever - did anyone want to participate or shoot with one, not even once or twice. One time, one of the nurses decided to join me, and we played "Asshole" or some shooting game like that.

AMELIA: Did you bother finding someone to play with you?

MARCEL: Yeah, a few times, but no one seemed interested enough. This one guy I knew would always say "Yes!" when I asked him, but when it came time he was always doing something else and couldn't peel himself off the chair.

AMELIA: (*Smiles*) But doing it alone seemed to help you anyway.

MARCEL: I found it to be really relaxing. Like Zen archery. If you keep thinking of the shot, it is bound to fail.

He asked her what happened to Regine, since he hadn't seen her in years, or at least the last time she and Amelia visited him. Amelia looked downwards the minute he asked it, and said that their friendship hit some rocky terrain when she flew out to Seattle with her Mother and Brother and went to school out there. She said that they exchanged messages infrequently and phone calls even more infrequently; it was terribly unfortunate. "We talk, but it's strained." Last she heard, Regine was interested in Physical Therapy, like her Mother.

When Amelia wasn't around, which was often, Marcel found himself wandering around the house, totally aimless, and taken with reading all of the books in the family library, growing withered in the living room and woefully unread. Some of them were only partially cracked - Lucile was forced at gunpoint to read *The Great Gatsby* for school - and his Father's meager books on cars and 'relaxation procedures' was on display. Marcel's Mother didn't read much - she showed an interest in books on art and so for Christmas he bought her a massive hardbound book of the complete works of Francesco Clemente and another on Franz Kline whose aching simplicity - black on white - delighted her eye but to Tom Wolfe, ships from outer space couldn't penetrate. Maybe Kline's Mother was right all along: he did find the easy way out. Simple or not, his work from Wilkes-Barre was appreciated.

Continuing the task of self-education was a challenge for Marcel, although one he started and was determined not to let up on. The education system forces one to read and learn things one does not want to - when one wants to laze about with friends and smoke and drink and laugh - so since Marcel was denied that forced learning by an external source - what learning he had before was 'laughable' - he had to maintain his own self-discipline and force himself to learn what others did. That was one of his fears: that he did not know as much as everyone else - that he was *substantially* inferior - and demanded that he try his best to catch up with them.

He never stayed too long on one subject, and tended to flip-flop eras; he would go from Dickens to Carver, from Civil War to Persian Gulf, from Agee to Bazin, from claptraps to jezebels. He didn't want to exhaust himself by taking too much of any one topic for too long, and didn't like stretching his reading in one genre or realm for more than three days - his self-education was to be slow and steady and varied. He frequented the library, where he became a regular - every week, Tuesday afternoon. The inherent deadline of having to return checked-out items taught him not to dawdle and made him anxious to get through one book he did not like (*Kon-Tiki*) and back into one he did (*The Count of Monte Cristo*).

His Father arranged for him to get a part-time job as a courier for Dr. Moore, a denture manufacturer, driving boxes of teeth to the various dentist offices around town, and when not doing that he would help Dr. Moore's secretary file paperwork and organize the office. He didn't mind the job or the hours - 8:30 AM to 1:00 PM - and it afforded him the opportunity to browse around Philadelphia, swerving through traffic, having his driving skills tested just a few months after getting his license and people watching all at the same time. He would see the girls from U. Penn soak up South Street, the Villanova guys marching around Market, the Temple students confined to their frightening campus, bars and all. While driving, he listened to sports radio religiously, and delighted in hearing the rabid townies bitch about the local teams struggling, anticipate who was going to win the football game on Sunday, contemplate who was going to be traded and countless other things (wives, children, pot holes, bosses, strange peanut recipes and new movies all got some time in-between), or engage in gossip about off-the-field shenanigans, talk about the slacker players not showing up for practice, dish dirt on whatever celebrity did not tip at a local restaurant or act belligerent in a local bar.

The afternoons were free, then, for lunch and meetings and reading and walking around the neighborhood with Mother or Father - whoever was home - and watching television with whoever was in the room (Marcel let everyone else handle the remote, more interested in seeing what catches their eye than choosing himself) and sporadically tooling around with the family computer. His social life, for the time being, was limited, and since communication with Amelia was so very infrequent, he made a point to talk to Lucile, who was having minor trouble in some schoolwork and didn't bother consulting their parents. Marcel seemed the safest possible bet, and while the two were sitting on the downstairs couches and going over her work, she would casually relay her day to him, mentioning altercations or disappointments -

arguments with friends, misinterpreted conversations. Not sure who all these new people were, Marcel made her go back to the beginning and add detail to the story from there, describing her involvement with these people, whether they had been friends before, whether they had been foes before or not on her same wavelength. He asked for minor descriptions of them, but she wasn't good at pointing out features or quirks - she'd rather pull out her yearbooks and show him older photos of her peers. From there - with their mug shot images upside down in the middle of his eyes and the gossip on each of them attached to their faces with paperclips - he tried to form an adequate representation of her circle and the circles around her, trying to experience her high school through her words, the high school of bodies stuffed in rooms and subsequently disassembled. Through discussion, Marcel was trying to form a common bond and understanding with this girl he never grew up with, this Sister of his he felt was a complete stranger. He offered advice and insight based on her descriptions and stories, and always tried to use logic and ethics - sometimes his responses wouldn't go over well and his theories would be thrown away instantly by her, sometimes with her belittling him at the end, saying something like, "What the hell do you know?" When she stormed away with her textbooks and pens in hand he tried to apologize but felt inside he hit a nerve with his statement because it was truthful ... but sometimes, his responses were half-cocked and too judgmental of Lucile.

When he asked for his Mother's help in redecorating his room, she offered the suggestion that Lucile help - she had a trickle of visual talent coursing through her and didn't put up a fuss when Mother asked her to help Marcel out. She also saw it as a way for them to work together and understand each other and compromise. Marcel didn't care much about the finished product or what it would look like, but the amethyst elephants on the trimming that was never scratched off needed to go, and the ceiling that had formed charcoal-like black lines running horizontally needed repainting.

It took the two of them about a week plus to revamp and putter with the room, sharing the painting duties and buying new, assemble-it-yourself furniture. Since they decided to work in the summer, they were able to keep the windows wide open to circulate the air. One of those days some carpeting people came to replace the shabby looking brown mess that was in place for about two decades with a new, plush one with a more colorful light blue tone. Once the carpet was in place, the men that installed it volunteered to help carry in the already-assembled dressers in the hallway. Their Father was covering the bill, and tipped the men a little extra and sent them off with cold sodas.

While they were busy rearranging and moving, Marcel also let his guard down, talking a little bit about himself, his experiences in the centers, the random yelling, the dead calm, the overwhelming anxiety - and in telling her those things, he hoped she would begin to understand and not condemn. He figured if she could talk about herself to some degree, it was only fair for him to return the favor and use the time to tell his own tale. He scanned her face for signs of empathy or compassion, but couldn't read anything: it was all in a null register, incapable, as of yet, to reveal outwardly what she thought. He felt there was a profound disappointment swimming in her head, shame even, and explained that it was okay to feel that way, that a lot of people feel that way about a lot of things they've done or people close to them have done. He admitted that he'd rather glaze over his own era as well.

Marcel's developing better rapport with Lucile became a point of discussion in part of his therapy meetings; he talked about their time together, their becoming better acquainted. The Doctor asked if Marcel felt she was a problem area in his life. The Doctor asked if Marcel felt his parents were a problem area in his life. The Doctor asked Marcel about his goals in life, and asked him to write down, on a sheet of yellow lined paper, all the things he wanted to do, no matter how small. Before the session was over, he wrote down four, but wasn't sure if they were the right goals the Doctor wanted him to have.

4.

Marcel found that work was a good distraction from some of his scattershot thoughts and fleeting fixations and continued interest in Daphne, who he looked for in every girl he saw. He anticipated waking up and working for Dr. Moore, but just a few months after he began his job, Dr. Moore started calling early in the morning and saying that there wasn't anything to do for the day, that business was getting slower, that the doctors were sending their secretaries and hired help to get the dentures (and other orders) and that his secretary had a good handle on the office - in other words, not to bother coming until needed. This prompted Marcel to talk to his Father about working for his seafood company, which *he* inherited from *his* Father. But Marcel's parents discussed it for some time and, for whatever reason, came to the mutual understanding that driving tractor-trailers out of state or even in state but for long distances wouldn't be the best thing to do for him at the present time - it was never explicitly mentioned, of course, but they didn't want to let him drive around pell-mell just yet, they didn't want him handling things like that so quickly. Marcel saw, during one of his Tuesday trips to the Library he frequented that they needed a checkout clerk and so inquired about working there. Marcel's Mother insisted that she needed to 'pull strings,' and so made a few phone calls to people she knew that had some sway and could get him in. After two separate interviews with two different groups of people, he was given the 8 to 4 job as a checkout clerk (and dabbled in computer maintenance early on - the checkout clerk position came later - but did not work out). This position allowed him to read voraciously.

In two months Amelia returned home, finished with school and saddled with debt and in the need for a job. Marcel was pleased to know she was back and accessible, though she seemed genuinely distraught at being finished with school - the Post-Graduation Breakdown. Along with her, he also was re-introduced, by Amelia, to Josef, older, less unkempt but just as bombastic emotionally as before. Marcel hadn't seen Josef for a long time, and didn't know that he and Amelia actually did keep in touch after school, even though the two of them went to different colleges (which so many people promise to do but fail on the promise: "KIT" is in every yearbook message: *keep in touch*) - the two of them became friends, in fact, while discussing the Marcel Controversy, with Josef making the leap from his own private lunch table to Amelia and friends' lunch table, and with the two of them dating for a brief period of time. Marcel was surprised to hear this - Josef was never mentioned by Amelia at all - but still delighted to know that they became good friends, and felt as if he had a part in their connection. Josef, like Amelia, was also hunting for a job.

As the relationship with Marcel and his Sister became more familiar and subdued, it also became terribly awkward, as there were some situations with the two of them that did not put Marcel in a comfortable state of mind. One such instance was when Marcel started using the house computer to download pornography (still images and videos), but needed the machine in his room. He had hauled it upstairs one day for what he termed "research reasons" one long weekend that the parents were out for a weekend trip to the Mohegan Sun to gamble, see a few shows and meet up with friends. Marcel and Lucile were "trusted" enough to be on their best behavior, and the warning was given that their Aunt may drop by and bring food or check on them. But Aunt Debbie wasn't to be seen or heard from, and the siblings made due. Marcel knew how to make chicken parmigiana and Lucile volunteered to help him - they both thought it would be healthier than pizza or fast food. No company was to be allowed in the house, either, but Lucile defied that by bringing over her friend Sara and Marcel promised not to bother either of them. They watched films downstairs while Marcel took time to amass a horde of free porn, which he had been restricted from doing earlier because of the PC's former location. He had to be careful to eliminate any traces of the content after the fact, so there was a slight edge to his escapade. Though his room door didn't have a lock, he slid a small carton filled with tennis balls over to block the doorway a little (he didn't play tennis - they were Lucile's but she didn't have any place to store them in her cluttered den). He didn't feel like moving any of his dressers, since they were all heavy and right where he wanted them. He also figured he'd be left alone.

He was by himself, too, for a long time. He sat in front of the machine completely naked and slathered with KY Jelly - the keyboard was a mess and he was going to rinse it off in the shower after he was finished with it. He predicted he would be at it for an hour, but the sheer volume of images and diversity was staggering and absorbing: he had seen magazines tossed here and there, in various people's houses (Josef inherited an old video cassette library from his older Brother when he got married and his wife didn't want him to have around; one afternoon, Marcel and Josef flipped through some of the titles and marveled at the formidable collection that was built up), but that was incomparable to what he found for free. It was the libido of humanity and the subconscious of culture - depictions of bondage were compelling in an oddly abstract, artistic manner, though deriving pure sexual satisfaction from watching someone confined and immobile wasn't possible for him, just as seeing cigarette burns, golden showers and who knows what else didn't appeal to him either - he wasn't old enough to have acquired such taste. When he scanned the online bulletin boards, he avoided topics and terminology that didn't sound eminently appealing.

The scrounging and surfing during his pleasure session stretched into the night, and he hadn't even known that Sara left an hour earlier or even what time it was. He left his room briefly to see what was happening - he tossed on a pair of shorts and a beige polo shirt just to have something on - and after a brief conversation with a tired Lucile, a glass of Lon Lon Milk and several caffeine tablets from the downstairs bathroom medicine closet, he was back in his room - although he neglected, in the return, to put the crate by the door and forgot to shut it completely. His extended session-indulgence - the first time he would be given the time and space *to* indulge - had left the room in a state of stale ghastliness, with soiled tissues, spilt instant coffee, smeared lubricant, paper towels and plates of half-eaten food and several unwashed glasses setting on the floor, on the dressers and near the monitor.

When Lucile did venture upstairs to sleep, she heard rustling and disembodied voices from his room, and she dared to exit her own room and peek in his, to see what the commotion was about. She knocked on the door, but the door wasn't seated, and it pushed open with her knock only to see Marcel - from the back - and the machine itself in the room - combined, a pungent disaster. She heard him dismiss her and tell her to go to bed, so she let the door go - it was cracked open only slightly - and shuffled out of the hallway and into her own room.

The next day, once he rolled out and the smell rolled with him, Lucile offered to help him take care of the room, picking up the garbage and washing the dishes while he washed the keyboard off in the shower. He carried the computer back downstairs and double and triple-checked that all incendiary content was removed. Nothing more was said about it.

Another instance came an undefined amount of time later, and involved Lucile's then second boyfriend, Ryan. The first boyfriend lasted for one week before he moved on to some girl Lucile couldn't stand - Marcel talked to her about it and tried to console her, telling her the things she wanted to hear and making her feel a little better about it. Boyfriend 1 was smooth and overly impressed with himself, taking on an obsessive interest in his attire and bracelets and clothes, while Boyfriend 2, Ryan, was more brooding and quiet and conservative in dress. When he would come over to their house, Marcel and him would get along fine, talking about the latest music, which was the only thing Ryan wanted to talk about (that and soccer, but Marcel had little knowledge of the sport).

MARCEL: Do you play in a band?

RYAN: Not really.

MARCEL: Are you working solo?

RYAN: I've been using my laptop to record some things and play them back to hear what it sounds like, and changing chords around. I come up with my own ideas and just go with them.

MARCEL: I thought everyone your age that was into music wanted to form a band. Don't you have friends that do this type of thing?

RYAN: Everybody wants to play guitar or be a lead singer, so finding keyboardists or drummers or bassists is tough.

MARCEL: Hey, did you ever hear Eno's *Another Green World*?

RYAN: Yeah, I don't like his later stuff, though.

MARCEL: How about Reich? Or Stockhausen?

RYAN: I'm not big on classical.
MARCEL: Miles? Monk?
RYAN: Don't care for jazz.
MARCEL: Oh. I just wondered.

Marcel's Mother pulled him aside one day and asked what he thought of Ryan. This question caught him off guard, because he never expected his Mother to ask for his opinion or advice in any matter regarding Lucile. Marcel felt it wasn't his business to suppose what kind of person Ryan was, and that all business between Ryan and Lucile was theirs alone. Marcel's Mother said that she was good at reading people, but Ryan came across as being blank, vague and his reticence to speak to be imposing, and that it was Marcel's right to pass judgment - or as she termed it, "have an opinion" - on him, that he was genetically similar to Lucile and therefore in his best interest. Marcel explained to her that he felt that, despite being all the adjectives she accurately described him as, Ryan was loquacious when it came to things he was interested in, and silent when not - Lucile, he reminded her, was also the same way, solipsistic and disagreeable and developing.

But what was going on with Ryan and Lucile got close and intense and Marcel's parents - his Mother being the vocal one - expressed a concern that Ryan was 'weighing her down'. He would bring her home late, he was always around, sitting on the couch, he smoked, he was a musician, he had his tongue pierced, he wore pants and jackets and hats with peripherals that jingle-jangled. He was playing the role he wanted to play. Marcel's Mother said she didn't want him around, that he was 'creepy.' Lucile snuck out. They grounded her. She refused to listen and stormed away. Things got a little out of hand.

Lucile often snuck Ryan into the house, and Marcel helped her. He found the idea of people sneaking around the house to be deliciously romantic, but also realized that if their parents found out, Marcel wouldn't receive any punishment or blame - he was not sneaking around, he was not defiant. He would help her get Ryan in the front door - or the back door if need be - and led him upstairs to her room. They'd shut the door, and Marcel would retire to his room and sleep with his ear to the wall, listening to the slightest sounds. Getting Ryan out of the house was always Lucile's responsibility.

Occasionally, he would see the two of them touching on the sofa in the living room. If he'd been smart and economical he would have used the family camcorder - which was swiped by Marcel a while ago from the downstairs closet and stored in his bedroom closet and tinkered around with periodically - to record them and use it as blackmail or something worse, but didn't, and also realized that blackmailing her would be the worst possible thing he could do and the least profitable thing he could do. When he did catch them close on the sofa or floor when their parents went out to dinner without them or were both working, he didn't bother them; in fact, he provided surveillance sometimes, peering out the upstairs window to see any cars coming in the driveway. If he spotted their encroaching vehicles in time, he yelled downstairs and Ryan was shoved out the back door.

5.

Marcel was laid off from his library job because of problems with state funding - apparently, books and personnel and self-education were not high on the agenda (though presumably, the more abstract 'education' was - constant headlines in the local paper spilled rivers of ink over how much the Governor was giving for education, how important students were, how vital it was that teachers trained and trained). So once he was sent walking and collecting through unemployment he found himself roaming around the house, anxious, making phone calls to Amelia or just talking to his parents. Amelia told him she took a job as a waitress at Petrillo's Steak and Grill for 'just the time being' to save up money. Tired of being at home, too, she began working with a local theater group to learn the craft and dabble around. It was there that she - and a friend of hers named Cameron that she met at a party at Villanova (where she and her friends went on a whim one night) - started spending a good amount of their non-working time. Amelia invited Marcel to come and watch the rehearsals for a new production they were hoping to put on based on a stage play one of the actors whipped up about two Sisters who fight over this boy in their school, and what happens when the boy picks the more attractive Sister and how the other Sister tries to interfere. Based on what Marcel was able to see - sitting in the seats virtually alone and gently sipping on his soft drink - the actors and meager crew couldn't make up their mind on any of the minor staging issues and spent their time bickering about lighting and dialogue.

Afterwards, Marcel, Amelia and Cameron went out for some Belgian beer to discuss it. It gave Marcel a chance to meet Cameron.

MARCEL: I never knew you had any desire to act or do that type of thing.

AMELIA: I took a few classes in college - the first two classes you take for acting - and it caught on. I had fun doing it.

CAMERON: I told her to do it.

AMELIA: (*Laughing*) You told me *not* to do it!

CAMERON: But now you do it and enjoy it. (*Pause*) You're so very welcome.

MARCEL: None of you seemed to know what you were doing, but it was fun to watch.

CAMERON: Oh, we're terrible. The writer wants to be a director, too.

MARCEL: Is there a director?

CAMERON: It was decided early that we'd direct as a collective, but that idea was horseshit.

AMELIA: (*Grins*) We're just a step above dinner theater, so the whole 'do-it-ourselves thing' isn't the wisest move.

CAMERON: It costs money to put on other people's plays, and doing something that no one's heard of does have its benefits.

Marcel enjoyed meeting Cameron and actually took up his and Amelia's offer to watch them rehearse every so often since he had nothing else to meddle with for the time being. A few times Josef stopped in to take a look after he got out of work at 4 PM - he landed a position at one of the local banks and was doing some basic database work - and one time Lucile was curious enough to want to go along (Marcel warned her that she may not like sitting around, seeing people argue and flub their lines, but she insisted so he took her). Josef didn't have that much to do during the day and was there to add "moral support" (his visits were brief - he never stayed until the end - but pleasant; he returned to his hovel thereafter for soup, coffee and several hours of watching *Heimat I* on video cassette). When practice was over, they'd go for drinks and socialize 'til all hours - more than once they'd close the bar they were at. Shuffling home at all hours of the night was not going over well with Marcel's parents, and the fact that they thought he was drinking - a big problem considering his prescription intake - was also cause for alarm (he usually had one beer and that was it, but they said he shouldn't have any).

His psychiatrist advised against the drinking strongly, warning of potentially harmful side-effects and health risks, and Marcel nodded and told him it was fine, under control, stabilized. Marcel's economic status was not so stabilized and he complained about losing his cushiony job at the library, which he enjoyed. Marcel expressed an interest to work for his Father's company, but wasn't sure in what capacity - the Doctor saw nothing wrong with that but suggested he take it up with his family during dinner.

His family was at first confused, then argumentative, when first broached with the concept - Marcel did not see it as that big a deal, but Marcel's Father wondered aloud to what capacity could Marcel assist? Follow him around all day? Aid his secretary? Marcel had an idea: why not be one of the drivers? Make deliveries? Deskwork didn't interest him in the least; he loved to be on the roads and outside. He liked his job as a courier for Dr. Moore, and the opportunity to roam was what really interested him. The 'rents held a private conference; he retreated to his room to read.

Their conclusion was that the idea wasn't half-bad, and that it wouldn't be a financial burden for him as long as he paid Marcel a portion of what he paid his regular drivers. It was set up that he would first go to driving school and then he could begin work - his Father volunteered to take care of the bill, which was considerate, since Marcel needed his unemployment checks for car insurance and other basic needs. Lucile had no response when Marcel informed her of his plan - she only looked through him. He explained it might be different; it was better than nothing. She said not a word. He felt like he had to rationalize to her his intention to try things out. She asked if there were other libraries for him to apply at. He quickly said no.

After the eight week course for his Commercial Driver's License and the streams of paperwork, and given some specific instructions and a trial run by his Father, Marcel was ready to start doing the deliveries and dealing with the daily grind of traveling short distances. He was introduced to some of the people involved in the operation - people he'd met only intermittently when they visited his house: George and Teddy (or names similar to those), his Father's secretary Sally, and some stragglers pacing up and down the asphalt in blue jeans and tan boots. His Father was gracious and patient with him - showing him how to load and unload, shelving techniques, safety rules, general procedure and protocol - and though Marcel knew a lot of the things he was being told, he listened and followed and agreed. Marcel worried about how everyone else would view his being there, and worried about being an embarrassment to his Father. But his Father didn't act embarrassed or uncomfortable: he was purely professional.

Marcel was given mostly simple runs at first - taking various orders to places he could get to within an hour. Sally would provide directions and a backup road map just in case. The drives were scenic and uncluttered - whenever possible, he was advised to avoid major highways - and he didn't waste time getting to his destination either; he wanted to be regarded as timely, dependable and responsible. His Father was fairly lenient, and as long as the little work given to him was sufficiently handled and he didn't "give anyone a hard time" (which was something he tried his best not to do; when faced with potential difficulty or was greeted with fury, he self-consciously spoke low, spoke slow and didn't say very much). He took to driving exceptionally well and shuddered internally when he realized he was probably more mechanically-oriented than artistic or intellectually acute: he would have rather been the latter of the two, and put on a good show for the paying audience, assembling his own Faustian knowledge database, but neither God nor Mephistopheles were gambling for his soul - in a sense, his time to develop those latter two skills had passed (or more accurately, the timeframe for him to develop those latter two skills was dwindling) and it wasn't something he wanted to accept or contemplate.

He discussed matters with Josef, Amelia and Cameron over drinks (he had a coffee):

AMELIA: What do you make of the trucking business?

MARCEL: There is something to being able to see people doing things you yourself are not doing: you're watching the business men and women in their suits and dresses with their briefcases and purses doing the daily walk into monstrous buildings or private offices. I feel like I'm window-shopping, in a weird way. I'm surrounded by images. And they're more varied than most teachers see, retail workers see, the monitors programmers see, the desks and workbenches engineers see.

JOSEF: At the bank, I don't even get to see any customers because my desk is in the back room. I don't even get to touch the money.

AMELIA: Didn't you mention something before that you were applying to graduate schools?

JOSEF: My friend Terrence and I are, yeah. So many people say that they want to go back to school but wind up working, make plans, get lost in their lives and stuck in long-term relationships and never do it. So we filled out the applications, got the transcripts rolling and now we're just waiting to see. (*Pause*) I think he's got a better chance than me - I slipped up here and there - and now it's wait and see time.

CAMERON: How does the bank pay?

JOSEF: (*Waves hand*) So-so. I can stand it for now, but if it were my life calling I'd lose my mind.

(*Pause. Josef excuses himself to go to the bathroom*)

MARCEL: How are you feeling about your play's upcoming opening night?

AMELIA: I'm scared.

CAMERON: I'm more scared than you.

MARCEL: You've all improved so much since you began that it should go fine. People aren't expecting miracles. At least you aren't doing surrealist stuff like this guy Arrabal that Josef was telling me about, which people have trouble digesting.

Opening night was two days after they had that conversation, and because of the theater's following - lots of locals supporting small productions, which was always good to see - all the seats were sold out. Marcel bought four tickets and drove Josef, Lucile and Ryan, who all wanted to go (even Ryan felt it was a pleasant diversion from *his* usual Friday Night although everyone knew he was going because Lucile wanted him to go). Marcel was slightly worried about how bored Lucile and Ryan would be, and made a point to tell them about how they might not like it and that no matter what, always be kind to the cast afterwards when they mingled with the crowd.

A genuine critic would have had a field day taking apart the amateur play's mechanics - its various symbols were overused (one character clutches and frequently speaks to a toy doll), the character development was lacking in substance and the story wasn't explicitly defined - issues already thought to be resolved between two of the characters in a parking lot are brought back two scenes later as if the earlier scene never existed. The actors, however, were genuinely enthused and passionate about being on stage, and the infectiousness kept the audience alert and attentive. Cameron, to Marcel, had really grown into the character and steered clear of the line reading-type delivery and mechanical movement of his early experiences - his particular role was that of a slimy conniver, so he needed to be more Mickey Rourke than Gary Cooper. Amelia was delightful to see, as well, and though some of the same annoying tics she displayed during the rehearsals kept reappearing on stage - like her tendency to subtly roll her shoulders when speaking, her using her arms in a circular motion when expressing rage, her overuse of the eye-roll to register disgust - but these observations Marcel had been making all along were never released from his head: he sat quietly and watched and judged, and that judgment had come from comparing Amelia to, say, Myrna Loy or Irene Dunne. He was no expert, just a hobbyist, at the risk of offending his friends, he let them work out their own kinks and served as a giant emotional pillow.

After the play was over, the cast received a warm standing ovation from an appreciative crowd. Lucile and Ryan were standing as well, and reading their faces he figured they had a decent time. Out in the lobby, the cast had come out to speak with and thank everyone and potentially get on good terms with important types or just receive accolades from pleasant folk, theater fans, or artsy-types with good intentions that talk a really good game and seem impressed by everything. Cameron invited Marcel et. al. to the after-after party, but Marcel declined and Josef made some excuse about needing some rest. Marcel was also responsible for Lucile and Ryan, and took Ryan home first.

For the next three weekends the play showed - Fridays, once; Saturdays, twice; Sundays, twice - Marcel was at all of them but one (the second Saturday morning he had to make a delivery for his Father that was considered "urgent" thereby missing the matinee but still rushing to catch the 8 PM). He made it a point to study the movements, the motion, the performances - he made an important note to himself that the actors and actresses do improve with each showing, as they work and work, that betterment - in this case - came from repetition. Within no time he knew their lines and knew the stage directions; if he subdivided multiple times, his cell-replicas could have done the production as well as they could. Someone in the cast jokingly gave him a generic #1 Fan t-shirt which he appeared grateful for receiving but disposed of by throwing it in his Father's t-shirt drawer.

Weeks after the play had run its course and was disbanded (no one intended to take it farther), Cameron and Amelia were itching to go with something new, and were trying to get together with several people to assemble some sort of production - they didn't care what it was either, names or no names, just as long as it was something to do. They wanted to keep going, keep practicing and gaining experience, but not many opportunities were available because not that many theaters were in the city. Josef correctly observed that most of the new plays coming out in the city were being put on by the local colleges, which logically left all non-students out.

In another six weeks' time, close to May, over drinks, Josef paid for everyone's tab in celebration of his being accepted to Tulane University in Louisiana. His friend Terrence, was also going there, and the two planned to share an apartment. He felt that there wouldn't be any competition between them since they'd both be studying different subjects, and since Josef never lived outside Pennsylvania he was a little hesitant to move so far away alone. He told everyone that Terrence was also accepted by the University of Texas at Austin, but Terrence claimed they were low-balling him in terms of financial aid. He told everyone he'd be leaving early - around mid-July - to get accustomed to the area and familiarize himself with places he would need to get to and adjust to the scenery. Everyone congratulated him on his good fortune, and wished him luck early. His bill for the night was over $250, but he did not flinch.

6.

On a long Friday that Lucile had off from school (Teacher In-Service day, mid-month), she asked Marcel if she could go with him on one of his delivery runs and see what it was like. He said no, it would be boring for her, but she insisted, and he continued to refuse. She asked their Father if she could, and he didn't see anything wrong with her going. So once the mandate came down, Marcel relented and took her along as his very first co-pilot.

He showed her all the details of what he does - occasionally helping to load the tractor-trailer, checking the temperature gauges, checking in with the office. Sally thought it was very amusing that Marcel had to play chauffeur and made some comment about not losing her along the way. The shipment was going to Wilkes-Barre, and Marcel warned that it might be much later until they got back to Philly, so she couldn't spend the afternoon with Ryan. She didn't mind, and Ryan was busy with something-or-other so he wasn't a factor.

He feared that he would have to entertain her or else the cabin would be quiet, not sure what to say or worried she was bored or disinterested or regretful that she went along. But once they went on their way, she was verbose and content, talking about herself, her friends, her week, and complaining about some odd gesture Ryan tended to make by tugging at the front of his pants that everyone would notice and silently giggle at. She demanded this cease at once.

LUCILE: We haven't had a lot of time to talk recently. You've been too busy.

MARCEL: I can't help that.

LUCILE: I thought you were mad at me.

MARCEL: (*Taken back*) Why would I be mad?

LUCILE: I don't know. Your being oh so quiet, maybe.

Lucile talked about how she wasn't sure if college was right for her, her pressures at school, looming graduation, moving on. She talked about one of her newer friends, Kathleen - a girl she didn't like for years, but now seemed to get along with.

MARCEL: Did I ever meet her?

LUCILE: No. We have study hall. It's - all right. She's been all over the world and acts superior to everyone, but for some reason everyone's impressed.

MARCEL: She acts rudely to everyone and gets away with it?

LUCILE: Yeah. (*Pause*) She's pretty, too. The guys are after her. She's going out with this guy she met that's a year older than her. I don't know where he goes to school. (*Pause*) I met him once. I didn't think he was much to look at.

MARCEL: As long as she's nice to you.

LUCILE: We talk about a lot. (*Drifts off*)

MARCEL: The other kids?

LUCILE: Yeah, them. (*Smiles*)

MARCEL: Aren't the guys after you?

LUCILE: (*Pause*) No. Not really. Well, two guys, I think. I'm not sure. Someone told me about the one guy. He's okay. The other guy's really into cars. It's sick. He washes it right after he drives it.

MARCEL: A lot of people like cars.

LUCILE: It's so ridiculous. It just takes you from one place to another.

MARCEL: You just don't know a lot about them.

They chatted for some time about their parents, overheard conversations between them, complaints (the basement and attic were filled to maximum capacity with junk and should be cleaned out), personal grousing (Lucile expressed concern that their Father has a gambling problem but Marcel didn't believe that at all) and general rambling about popular culture. After an extensive period of silence following the outburst, Lucile summoned the courage to resume:

LUCILE: Can I ask you a personal question?

MARCEL: (*Surprised*) About what?

LUCILE: You.

MARCEL: I'm not sure.

LUCILE: Not sure if you want me to ask or not sure if you want to answer?

MARCEL: Yes.

LUCILE: So you don't want me to ask. I won't.

MARCEL: No, go ahead.

LUCILE: If it's....

MARCEL: You have to now that you brought it up.

LUCILE: Okay. (*Pause*) What made them let you out?

MARCEL: (*Perturbed*) 'Let me out?'

LUCILE: Yeah.

MARCEL: You make it sound like I was in prison.

LUCILE: You were, in a way.

MARCEL: I didn't do anything wrong.

LUCILE: But how did you get out?

Marcel took time to ready his answer.

MARCEL: Why didn't you ask me this a long time ago?

LUCILE: Mom and Dad said not to, that you were fine and that you didn't want to talk about anything. Dad said it's like Vietnam and something you just brush away like it never happened.

MARCEL: And now you feel as if it's the right time.

LUCILE: Better now than never?

MARCEL: (*Takes deep breath*) I, well, I guess they think that I bettered myself by staying there, that I didn't need them to watch over me anymore, that their treatment worked, and that I wasn't doing any good in there. Plus, they were turning me over to Mom and Dad, who are still basically my caretakers.

LUCILE: You've been calm.

MARCEL: I feel pretty good, actually.

LUCILE: What did they do to you?

MARCEL: What do you think they did?

LUCILE: I don't know anything about it.

MARCEL: It was like I was in a dormitory. I had special classes and read books and took tests and we had exercises we had to do. We watched films on Friday and Saturday. We met with doctors, physicians. We watched television. I read and watched television most of the day.

LUCILE: Are you mad Mom and Dad put you there?

MARCEL: (*Shrugs*) I don't know if that's the case. I honestly don't remember or know all the details from back then. It gets me nowhere being mad at them. I did learn later on that they actually wanted me to be there, that they were convinced it would benefit me, and they made a decision. I don't know, if I had children that had difficulty in life and were problematic, what to do for them? To keep bouncing them from building to building? To ignore it? It's over.

LUCILE: I thought you were never going to leave.

MARCEL: Sometimes I thought I was never going to leave. I would see people leave all the time. It's a steady influx. Some come, some go, some move.

LUCILE: You never talk about anybody you met there.

MARCEL: There isn't much to say.

LUCILE: You have to have something to say.

MARCEL: I should ... but, it was like I was sitting on a bench on a busy street. Sometimes, someone would sit next to me, and this person would sit quietly before standing up and walking away and sometimes another person would turn and talk on and on as if everyone was listening to them. And all the while you're sitting and either nothing is being said or everything is being said, there are people passing by right in front of you that you watch pass by you - people who won't sit next to you and who have someplace they have to go. I got so tired of watching people pass in front of me, that I started reading so I didn't have to watch them and I wasn't obligated to the person sitting next to me in any way. By the time they got to me, their stories were already half-finished or just fragments, and I wasn't sure where it began or what it meant. I lost the urge to care.

LUCILE: Sounds sad.

MARCEL: It isn't, really. They weren't sad, and neither was I. They were talking for themselves, and the people walking in front of me were doing their own thing. I was doing my thing, occupying myself.

It was decided that after the delivery was made and all the paperwork was printed up and finalized and they were driving back home from Wilkes-Barre, that they would pull off to the side of the road at some rest stop or parking lot and eat their packed lunches that Lucile had thrown together (Marcel had suggested that they splurge and just eat out, but Lucile was too weight-conscious for fast food or diner meals).

MARCEL: You're not fat.

LUCILE: But I can be if I don't watch.

MARCEL: Mom and Dad aren't fat. I'm not fat.

LUCILE: What does that mean?

MARCEL: It means genetics. You're not genetically created to be heavy.

LUCILE: Eating better is good for your long-term health. Skinny people can have serious health problems, too.

MARCEL: You're too young.

LUCILE: Early awareness circumvents future hazards. See your doctor or call our toll-free number.

MARCEL: (*Rolls his eyes, smiles*) Good heavens. You'll burn it off.

Marcel left it up to Lucile to pick their lunching spot, since she had coordinated the meal-thing from the beginning. After steam rolling through an Industrial Park in one of the towns they were traversing, she advised he pull into this large, completely abandoned parking lot owned by a company named Middleton. The entire surrounding area was quiet, the roads were quiet and all the lights were out inside the generic gray buildings. Marcel parked the tractor-trailer at an angle and in the dead center of the lot. Lucile sorted through the brown bags.

She handed him his personalized lunch bag. Inside it was:

> 1 tuna fish on whole wheat bread, toasted, with
> lettuce and tomato
> 1 travel pack of honey-flavored graham crackers
> 1 plastic bag filled with washed green grapes
> 1 plastic bag filled with cut celery sticks
> 1 white folded napkin
> 1 travel box of Lon Lon 2% Milk with a small
> flexible straw

MARCEL: This is a very nutritious meal you made for me. What's in yours?

LUCILE: The same, except mine has Lon Lon Apple Juice and chocolate wafers instead of graham crackers. Want to trade?

Marcel declined, and they sat in the tractor-trailer and scanned the area for little details and points of temporary interest while they ate. Since it was Saturday, it afforded them a nice place to relax. Being in no hurry to return back home, Marcel slowly consumed his meal. Having finished well before him, Lucile started in with more questions.

LUCILE: So, what's going on between you and Amelia?

MARCEL: Nothing.

LUCILE: She likes you.

MARCEL: And I like her.

LUCILE: Are you two dating? Or is Cameron dating her?

MARCEL: I'm not dating her. Neither is Cameron. They're just friends. We're just friends.

LUCILE: But I see you and her together a lot. It's more than that.

MARCEL: No it isn't. I like her, she likes me, but otherwise we're incompatible, same with her and Cameron. You're thinking too far ahead.

LUCILE: But wouldn't you want to date her?

MARCEL: If she was a different type of person and I was a different type of person, sure, why not.

LUCILE: (*Pause*) Ever think about marriage?

MARCEL: Absolutely.

LUCILE: And?

MARCEL: It might work if the right situation arises.

LUCILE: (*Pause*) Aren't you too old to be living at home?

MARCEL: Is there an age that says you have to leave? I'm doing okay. I'm not old.

LUCILE: Yes you are.

MARCEL: Let's see where you are when you're my age.

LUCILE: (*Smiles*) I'll be out.

MARCEL: (*Scoffs*) Swallow your tongue. You know nothing right now.

LUCILE: Josef agrees with me.

MARCEL: Josef?

LUCILE: I asked him and he agreed.

MARCEL: When was this?

LUCILE: A while ago. On the phone. I asked him what a good age to be out of the house and on your own should be. He said twenty-one should be the limit.

MARCEL: Josef lives at home.

LUCILE: He's too old to be at home too, then.

Marcel drank the rest of his milk and stuffed the garbage back into the brown paper bag and set it aside. Across the street he saw three bicyclists wearing bright yellow shorts and bright yellow shirts on their matching bright yellow bikes streaming down the road, to their left, one right after the other. Both he and Lucile stared at them, momentarily immobile. After they passed and were out of sight, he started up the engine. He let it run, allowing it to warm up.

Lucile kept talking. She went on about herself, about Marcel, and kept on with the questioning process. Marcel remained silent, tired of addressing her and encouraging her to continue.

LUCILE: What do you think we should do with you if you become a problem again?

MARCEL: Put me down.

LUCILE: I'm being serious.

MARCEL: So am I.

LUCILE: But you aren't.

MARCEL: What do you want me to say? I'd rather not go into it all.

LUCILE: I'm just trying to get you to be truthful for once.

MARCEL: (*Louder*) I am being truthful. Maybe you just aren't *listening* close enough.

LUCILE: (*Looking down*) … Hmm.

MARCEL: (*Pause*) Is the reason you came with me today to have a friendly talk or to interrogate? Do you badger your friends like this? Maybe that's why you don't have many.

LUCILE: (*Shrugs*) I'm just interested.

Minutes passed and neither said a word to each other. Lucile sat looking out her side window. Marcel glanced over to her every so often to check on her, but she didn't move. After a few miles, he tried to break the silence.

MARCEL: I'm sorry.

He turned his head briefly to look. She still didn't respond.

MARCEL: Why don't you just feed me the lines you want me to say? Tell me what words you want to hear, because I'm not sure what you want to know. Tell me what responses I should give you. (*Pause*) Go on. (*Pause*) Line them up. (*Pause*) Where are they? Where are the questions? Where's the term paper?

She didn't even flinch. She sat motionless. As a direct result, he stopped trying to speak to her. He figured he'd drive her back, take her home, and then let her work out her snit in a couple of days. This method works with almost everyone: give people space and they'll break down. Leave them alone and they'll crawl back. Treat them poorly and they'll work twice as hard to be kind to you. Let them know you don't need them and they'll want you more.

7.

Amelia and Cameron invited Marcel and Josef to take an Acting Workshop class with them; they thought their interest in the theater might translate into a desire to actually participate. Josef immediately declined, offering a cryptic excuse about it being "too nerve-wracking" and not having the time. The class was run by a local woman who had traveled all over the world, talked to different performers and learned from many instructors. She had no famous credentials and no one had ever seen her perform, but through the accumulation of experience - she boasted of her extensive resume - and age granted her 'old sage' status, and besides, it was only $99 for three days. Marcel was hesitant at first, but decided, eventually, that he might learn something valuable.

The woman that ran the class, Brenda, was in her late fifties, gaunt, wore a black turtleneck, black jogging pants and nodded incessantly whenever anyone said anything, ever, even if it was right or wrong. If someone needed to have a vital question answered, if he or she had to be excused to pee, if someone tripped and fell while walking across the floor, it was all nodding. This seemed like a perverse physical tic for someone who spent her entire life trying to remain perfectly still and in character, though Marcel figured it was her way of trying to be interested in the idiosyncrasies and odd questions and painful mistakes of her pupils who sought approval. Of the fifteen people in the class (not counting Cameron, Amelia or himself), he figured most were in it just to get out of the house, dabble and try something new.

Brenda paired people off to work on a good deal of the exercises and since Marcel was always left out he wound up with her. He didn't mind, however, and he'd rather work with someone who knew what she was trying to do versus someone else in class who was trying not to appear foolish. A great deal of the exercises attempted were seemingly dumb, from making nonsense noise (while looking into the face of your partner) and keeping a stern, cold appearance, to larger, more conceptual pieces, like walking outside of the room, then back in, and pretending to notice things in the room that were not there (a table, a chair). Marcel felt immensely silly doing these things himself, but he did his best to pretend he was putting on his best effort.

After the first day, Amelia and Cameron suggested they trade off - the next day, prospectively, Amelia would go with Brenda and on the third Cameron. Both figured he wouldn't want to be with her all the days, but he declined their offer, and said something about needing the most help.

Days two and three of the workshop had the class doing calisthenics in the beginning, the group exercises (standing in a circle and calling out other people in the circle's name, who would then call out another name, etc. - a kind of verbal hot-potato), odd facial activities (exaggerated smiles, exaggerated laughing) and interspersed between all of these, Brenda's theories on the art of performing, as well as Brenda's recounting her own personal history. Marcel felt as if she had been doing small, short classes of that sort for a while by the cautious planning and execution of the one he was taking part in - no one cobbling an interactive seminar like that for the first time could be as smooth-running and as time-efficient as she. The class discussed acting concepts like "rhythm" and "focus" as well as generic terminology like what are "heroes" and "heroines," "protagonists" and "antagonists."

One of the most pressing issues to Marcel was his inability to critique himself from the viewpoint of being a participant, and thought about the outsider's duty and obligation to provide assistance and aid, shape and mold. Likewise, Marcel's failure to self-modify left him at the mercy of others during the three-day workshop; when he asked Brenda what he should do in Situation X, and if what he did was incorrect, she would nod and offer positive advice - she criticized while surrounding the criticism with positive points. He felt horribly ashamed of his attempts to do some of the things he was asked, and feared being mocked in silence - and had not once (that he could tell) been snickered or mocked openly by his classmates, for he figured that they were most likely afraid they'd looked foolish themselves. This rationale did not completely satisfy him, but he pressed on nonetheless.

On the third day, for the final segment of class, all of the students had to go up in front of everyone and do a little number, alone: deliver a small monologue that had been picked out for each individual by Brenda. Marcel was handed a two-page bit from *Death of a Salesman*, and he was Biff to Brenda's Happy (Brenda, seated, mouthed the lines to her part). While his peers were going up and doing their routines - he could hardly care who or what they were doing - he pored over the pages and tried to study his lines well ahead of time, so he wouldn't have to rely on the photocopies too much. He wanted to go up there and look presentable and confident. When he was finished - he was second from last - he had heard her give some tips and remembered her corrections (don't slouch, think 'desperate,' enunciate, don't ramble) but at the end the inability to accurately measure how he did in comparison to everyone else in the class - how he ranked - bothered him. When he asked Cameron and Amelia (Josef dropped by later) over for dinner, they said he looked "better than they did" and basically refused to offer feedback, instead wondering what he thought of them. He remained mute and changed the subject; he did not want to admit he was so absorbed in his own foibles he couldn't concentrate on anything else.

Lucile's quiet phase had gone on for some time after the Saturday drive she took with Marcel and their brief but harsh conversation, and for that time the two of them never got around to just talking and making amends. Everyone in the family had noticed that Ryan wasn't calling or making impromptu visits, and any mention of him was forbidden. Marcel had been occupying himself with work, reading and various appointments like, for example, his mandatory yearly physical and meetings with a new Doctor (who had taken over his old Doctor's clientele but worked in the same professional building as him for years).

For the most part, Marcel felt well and kept active - he started a small jogging program for himself where he traveled from his home and went around the neighborhood - but found trouble following the regimen he established for himself, continuously straying off the schedule he penned into his Philadelphia Eagles wall calendar. He had contemplated asking Lucile to accompany him, but she was giving everyone a bad time - prompting their Mother to ask "When is she going to lighten up?" - and was left to start it and neglect it on his own. Mother and Father were rapidly becoming out of shape and gorging on meat and cheese - but without the wine - so they had no interest in Marcel's *Prefontainism*.

When Marcel's parents planned for a Spring Vacation to Lake George to relax and take a breather, they hadn't intended on taking either Marcel or Lucile along. Marcel decided at the last minute he wanted some time away from Philly, but his parents were resolute and appeared mock-apologetic, saying they already had their room booked two months prior (both said they had no idea he'd even had a small desire to go), and had to leave him home and act as care taker for Lucile (which was intended to make him feel responsible). Packed and armed with disposable cameras and minor provisions, they left at 7 AM on a Thursday, intending to return Sunday afternoon to late evening. Lucile refused to voice her disgust with them and only gave them a half-hearted wave goodbye, and Marcel was still in bed when their car flew out of the driveway.

Marcel made sure to plan ahead for himself while they were away, since he had no work and no responsibilities for the interim (it was a home-bound vacation for him; no Father at work, no work from Father). He yanked the family personal computer free from its resting spot and hauled it back upstairs - it wouldn't be until much later in the day that he would use it. He decided to spend his afternoon doing some light running, then some television time, then computer time and finally out with friends for dinner and drinks. He didn't want to clash with Lucile, so he decided she could fend for herself - she did, after all, get off to school on time in the morning.

Once Marcel got home from his two hour jog at close to 2:00, he made himself lunch and read the *New York Times*, which his Father started getting delivered to the house because he said the local papers were all about "football and fashion." After lunch, he skipped television time for PC time, staring at the pulsating screen and feeling the chilled air from his half-cracked window tickling his moist skin. On this particular day he became fascinated with the mechanics of the ejaculate release and trajectory - it never followed a set path, it sometimes sprayed around haphazardly; it went off at strange angles and dribbled along the sides. Sometimes the orgasm felt magnificent, other times it was merely adequate (profoundly, the memory of what the orgasm felt like became erased seconds following the moment). The amount of semen produced, he noticed, was not always indicative of the amount of pleasure received from the sensation of the orgasm - sometimes the trickling squall of a minor trajectory equated with intense pleasure whereas the ejaculations that screamed out of the gate in a mad fury left only slightly pleasing feelings. The volume of fluid produced varied tremendously - it would go from soaking tissues and paper towels (*Two ply can't hold me*) to two or three drops. Viscosity and color, Marcel read, were based on diet, and he made some futile attempts in the past to write down what he ate during the day and examine the color, thickness and texture of his semen later on (or whenever he was afforded the time to get off). He kept the tallies in a notebook but found no real consistency among the numbers. Medication, he felt, might have had an influence in all aspects of the orgasm, so he had to take that into account as well.

He kept an eye on the clock for the time Lucile would come home so he could pry himself away from the computer, get showered, clean himself a little, go downstairs and then goof around watching sports highlights or classic television shows; he wanted to mend whatever rift had formed in their relationship and do a little fast talking so that she didn't just run off and ignore him. He realized that if they were on good terms their time together, over the weekend, would be more pleasant for him to deal with.

But it was another bad day, and her entry was quick and discomforting. Marcel, seated on the couch, tried to ask what happened with her day, how her friends were, how her classes went - just a barrage of friendly questions, one right after the other - and she just grumbled and groaned, sorted through the mail on the kitchen table, went through the refrigerator for a container of yogurt, grabbed a Pepsi and stomped upstairs to her bedroom and closed the door. He followed her up, and acted concerned about how "something might be the matter" and wondered, "how he could help" but the door was shut and locked and she said she was tired and needed to make some phone calls. He paced around, filled with a combination of parental concern and Brotherly rage - if he couldn't console her or get her to behave sensibly, he wanted to smack her. He did not get a response and did not smack her, so he ventured back downstairs and watched Josef's copy of Leo McCarey's *Ruggles of Red Gap* that Josef strongly recommended he see.

After a series of phone call exchanges, Marcel and Josef decided to eat dinner at a small-scale Thai restaurant (Josef recommended it and provided the directions) - Cameron was eating at home, since he started his beans-and-chicken recipe already and Amelia was (as always) at work - both said they'd catch up with them later for carousing and stumbling. While eating, they talked about *Ruggles of Red Gap* (Josef asked, intrigued, what he thought of Laughton's performance and Marcel admitted he, with a face that resembles an elephant's ass, was very good, though balked at what he termed the movie's 'sappiness'), Billy Wilder's script for *One, Two, Three* (Josef: "Cagney's delivery is not just good ... it's perfect. He's high on Coke and spitting out retorts"), Josef's time off from work ("You know how everyone says they aren't going back to school after they leave, then realize that the real world that John Mayer says doesn't exist *does exist* and is quite exhausting so then start to tell people they're going back but never find the time to do so because life is in the way? I learned from those people that you have to pounce and pounce early. And screw them, I can't stand working in a bank.").

MARCEL: But if you don't like banking, what do you mean to do with your degree ... which is in Business, right?

JOSEF: I'll stay in school, you know ... go on and get my doctorate in some related field. Do research. Maybe teach at a college. It might be worth it. I like interaction, the *laissez faire* aloofness.

MARCEL: Why … why don't you go to study film, which you seem to really love?

JOSEF: The area's flooded.

MARCEL: So you can be one of the many.

JOSEF: (*Shrugs*) Nah.

MARCEL: You seemed to have given up drawing, too. You were good at that, too.

JOSEF: It was a hobby, and hobbies don't guarantee you money.

Josef changed the subject.

JOSEF: If you're here, where is the Sis?

MARCEL: (*Groans*) I just left the house. She wasn't talking to me and I'm not begging her to be friendly.

JOSEF: So she's still at home? Does she have anything to eat? We could take her something.

MARCEL: She'll order something on her own. She can drive.

JOSEF: (*Pause*) What did you two fight about now?

MARCEL: We got into an argument a while ago. I thought it was nothing and that she'd get over it, but she's still not over it, and I think there's something going on with her boyfriend and school.

JOSEF: Did your parents say anything?

MARCEL: They're waiting for her to work it out.

JOSEF: They learned their lesson with you, huh? (*Grins*)

MARCEL: Yeah … true, true. She could have eaten with us. But she has friends and it's (*Waves hand*) … I don't know.

JOSEF: (*Gets out his phone*) Want to call her? You can use my phone.

MARCEL: She's probably not home. I'll talk to her later.

While leaving, Josef spoke of his plans for his Summer of Excess.

JOSEF: Dubbing this the Summer of Excess is ironic in that it, knowing us, won't be excessive in the least. It will be pensive and restricted. Or not. But that came to me the other day - that thought - that the Summer would ... no, *should* brim with Overkill.

MARCEL: I know I plan on taking it easy.

JOSEF: See, that's why I've got you here. I was going to talk to Cameron and Amelia, but I'll try you first. I'm leaving to go to Louisiana early and I was wondering if you wanted to stop down with me. I can set you up with a free room - or free sleeping space - and you and me and Terrence and whoever else wants to come can lounge about in New Orleans for as long as we need. It'll give you time away from your parents and here. It's a mini-vacation. What do you think?

MARCEL: When will this be?

JOSEF: Lessee, well, I'm not sure exactly. But I want to get there early August, late July. Terrence is taking all the furniture ahead of time, so I'll only need to bring a few items down there. You game?

MARCEL: (*Thinks*) I'll have to get back to you on it.

Marcel got back to his house around 2:30 in the morning (he and Josef did meet up with an understandably lethargic Cameron and Amelia for a night of walking and killing time) and made sure to eat some bread and drink some juice before going to bed because he felt a little nauseous from the five or six cups of coffee he had - plus the volatile Thai food from earlier in the evening. Lucile's door was shut and there were objects from her room strewn about the hallway and bathroom, but he didn't want to knock and wake her up or even know what was going on. Slightly surly and aching to rest, he went into his own room, tossed his clothes in the corner and crawled into bed with his socks on. He glanced over to his computer with a longing eye but was too exhausted to pry himself up. He pressed his ear to the wall to listen what was going on next-door and check if her television was on or music was playing softly. He heard nothing and rolled over.

An untold amount of time later, however, he was awoken by a soft whispering, a cracked door and a shadowy face looming over his that asked if he was asleep.

MARCEL: (*Softly*) I *was* asleep.

LUCILE: I heard you come in.

She knelt next to his bed and rested her elbows on the mattress.

MARCEL: What's going on?

LUCILE: Do you mind if we talk?

MARCEL: Can it wait 'til breakfast?

LUCILE: I want to talk now.

MARCEL: Okay.

(*Extended pause*)

MARCEL: … well?

LUCILE: You didn't tell me you were leaving earlier.

MARCEL: You were in a foul mood.

LUCILE: I had a rough week. I'm allowed to have a rough week.

MARCEL: Tell me about it.

LUCILE: I hate it there.

MARCEL: You'll be getting out of school eventually.

LUCILE: I hate my friends.

MARCEL: Oh.

LUCILE: They're fucking backstabbers.

MARCEL: (*Pause*) Where's Ryan at? I haven't seen him.

LUCILE: He's with someone else now.

MARCEL: A friend of yours, right?

LUCILE: She used to be.

MARCEL: (*Sighs*) That's so clichéd. Guys moving from one girl to her girlfriends. On talk shows that's all you see. It only hurts feelings, it keeps happening, it's human nature.

LUCILE: I didn't even really like him, either.

MARCEL: Hah. Then why were you sneaking him in all the time?

LUCILE: I didn't want to be alone.

MARCEL: Couldn't you have picked someone you did like, then?

LUCILE: The guy I like is ... I don't think he's interested. I know. He, I just don't get the feeling it would work.

MARCEL: Is he dating someone?

LUCILE: I think so. It's off and on.

MARCEL: Ryan was second best, then.

LUCILE: (*Sighs*) I can't go through another year.

MARCEL: You'll go on.

LUCILE: (*Pause*) So, what did all of you do tonight?

MARCEL: Talked. Ate. What's there to do?

LUCILE: Hm.

MARCEL: And you?

LUCILE: I watched the tape Josef gave you.

MARCEL: Did you like it?

LUCILE: Yeah, but why did Ruggles keep looking at the camera? That was annoying. And the ending is corny.

MARCEL: Josef was talking about the ending earlier. I think Laughton kept looking at the camera as a way of identifying directly with the audience - of breaking down 'that wall.'

LUCILE: It was good. Old, though.

MARCEL: I'm very proud of you for watching it.

LUCILE: I had no choice. The cable went out.

MARCEL: Hm.

Marcel fell back asleep while Lucile was still talking about something he couldn't stay conscious to understand, and then awoke a little later, only to find that during that span of time she fell asleep too, still kneeling, and with her head resting in between her folded hands. The room was slightly cool, and he intended to take the blanket that was on top of him and, in a very cinematic gesture, cover her with it to represent that he cared, but before he was able to move he unwillingly returned to sleep; the two of them looked soft, sweet and pleasantly adrift.

Her hair smelled like fresh apples.

8.

(The Impulse)

Amelia met with Marcel for lunch at a small coffee shop/deli called "Mostly New" that served a hearty homemade soup (bouillabaisse) and a pita (garden herb) combo that she lived for. Marcel had the same, and a glass of water. The Lunch Meeting was Amelia's idea.

AMELIA: I've been talking fairly regularly with a friend of mine, Naomi, who lives in San Francisco. Well, actually, she's not 'my' friend - she's a friend of a friend - but lately we've been getting close. I was introduced to her about a year ago by Bethany Rogers - the three of us did a little bit of drinking and talking and exchanged numbers but I figured I'd never hear from her again. But she called every once and a while to just talk, so I knew it was okay to call her. I told her about struggling out here and how sick I was of waitressing, and she suggested I make a visit out West; she has a room in her new home - her parents are very rich - and she said I could be more successful in a city known for their arts.

MARCEL: If you wanted to pursue acting, why not New York?

AMELIA: Too stuffy.

MARCEL: San Francisco isn't? You've never been there.

AMELIA: Neither have you. (*Pause*) Plus, it's free rent.

MARCEL: Seems awfully generous.

AMELIA: I know. I've asked dozens of questions about the whole thing - what about this, what about that, and she just blows it all off. She's a free spirit, as they say.

MARCEL: But you only met her once.

AMELIA: I know.

MARCEL: Does she act?

AMELIA: No. She did dance for a while, though.

MARCEL: I see.

AMELIA: And paint. A little.

MARCEL: Hey, well, our Mothers painted. Now all we have are houses filled with Wyeth replicas and temperas of wild life.

AMELIA: They're pretty bad, too.

MARCEL: I don't know about that. Your Mom did that great painting of the one barn. Remember that?

AMELIA: It's in her bedroom.

MARCEL: If she doesn't want it any more, tell her I'll take it.

AMELIA: I will, I will. (*Smiles*)

Marcel watched her wipe the side of the soup bowl with a napkin and subtly rearranged the plates in front of her.

MARCEL: Okay, so this Naomi … she doesn't have a job herself, right?

AMELIA: I think she works for her Dad when he needs her.

MARCEL: Her and I have one thing in common, then. Shame I don't have my own house.

AMELIA: Her Father's an architect.

MARCEL: I see.

AMELIA: And her Mother's on City Council.

MARCEL: (*Smiles*) Ohhhh….

AMELIA: So she's allowed to dabble here and there. No strings.

MARCEL: (*Pause*) Them that's got shall have, them that's not shall lose.

Marcel's soup was cold but he didn't want to bother the staff and ask for it to be warmed up. He really liked the deli - the music player always had on some elegant, obscure new album from some elegant, obscure new band and the walls were covered, in earnest, with vintage movie and concert posters and album covers. On shelves built into the walls stood action figures, stuffed animals and assorted trinkets and donated college memorabilia - UPenn mugs, Temple Owl plushies - not to mention sports ephemera - Sixers, Flyers, Eagles, Phillies all had their share of space. For each sport, the star player had a poster someplace, but the poster was in a plastic protector and was changed often: as with professional athletes, their glory days tended to be so stunningly brief and their careers so pathetically short: the hero of one day got traded the next. Bodies wore out, broke down, collapsed. In a town like Philadelphia - or any other that lives and dies with its athlete heroes - athletic failure is often and regrettable. Fans show little or no mercy: every game for every major sport, a packed stadium filled with critics so lashing they make Pauline Kael and Rex Reed seem temperate in comparison, slicing apart the athletic narrative, dissecting on-the-field/on-the-ice performances, ridiculing their talent. One of the benefits of being mid-flow - in the middle of the game - is that most no one says what they think to your face and the screams of the audience are muted - it's only after that you not only hear about it, but also read about it in the paper for days and days. The same goes for the movies, where critics of all shapes with different ideologies and concepts of *great cinema* proceed to cast judgment and devastate reputations in high-profile papers and magazines. Everyone reads the criticism, too, no matter how strongly they assert that they don't care. It matters. They care.

MARCEL: (*Thinking*) Do you miss playing basketball?

AMELIA: Mmm ... no. It's fun and everything, but I don't have the time any more.

MARCEL: There are women's leagues.

AMELIA: I'm too rusty and out of it. The passion for it just died with time.

MARCEL: Josef said the same thing about those drawings he used to be good at. I find it a struggle to do the slightest exercise routine I set up for myself.

AMELIA: It's amazing - you get so little free time when you work and the free time you do have you just waste on nothing.

Marcel glanced around the room to see who was also sharing lunch with them, but it was 1 PM on a Tuesday and the few people that were eating when they came in had left. Even the man at the counter in the back in a green apron had disappeared.

MARCEL: So, is Cameron going with you? To San Francisco?

AMELIA: I don't know. I mentioned it to him last week and he was somewhat apathetic. The whole idea of picking up and moving ahead just seemed foreign to him.

MARCEL: He's not doing anything here.

AMELIA: He's disappointing in a way. He used to be far more adventurous. Used to be. Now, he's just letting time slip.

MARCEL: But would this girl -

AMELIA: Naomi.

MARCEL: Right, right, would she mind if he came along?

AMELIA: He's in the same situation I am. It would be good for him.

MARCEL: What about me?

AMELIA: You?

MARCEL: Why not?

AMELIA: What about your family? *Can* you go?

MARCEL: I've never been west of the Mississippi.

AMELIA: Right.

MARCEL: I've almost never been on a vacation or extended leave. It might be a blast. And since you'd be going there, I thought....

AMELIA: Right.

MARCEL: (*Softer*) I hope I'm not intruding. I hate to - wait, I'm intruding, aren't I?

AMELIA: Oh no. I just … didn't think you'd want to. Or would. I didn't think it was your thing. You never went anyplace with your parents before.

MARCEL: I am completely in favor of exploration and travel.

AMELIA: (*Smiles*) Is this a celebration of the 'new you?'

MARCEL: (*Shrugs*) It's the same old me. (*Pause*) How big is the house she has, anyway?

(The Action/Event)

Marcel and Josef put their ideas together into a metaphorical blender and concoct a scheme for everyone to follow religiously. It was heady and somewhat impulsive, but Marcel liked having something to look forward to doing, and if anything this was a successful way of getting his Planning Skills honed. Josef called it an "Action" that they were taking in commemoration of the Summer of Excess; Marcel referred to it as an "Event." Both were correct in their thinking, and both found it to be a delicious concept, conceived of by Marcel and built to spill by Josef, who sadly wouldn't be a Participant for what was the 'last part,' but volunteered to lend whatever extra assistance to the larger plan as necessary.

Josef made plans to go back to college early, which he informed everyone of and everyone understood. Josef was using his Grandmother's blue Saturn to drive to and from the bank, and had no vehicle to call his own. Josef asked Marcel if he would be willing to be the one to drive him down early in exchange for living quarters and gas money and Marcel was almost ready to accept his offer.

Marcel remarked how Amelia wanted to go out to California and see what was going on over there and how Cameron might accompany her. Marcel added that Amelia could come with them to Louisiana, then continue on and drive out West with Marcel. If Cameron wanted to come, he was invited. Marcel, if granted permission, would noodle around San Francisco and its surrounding areas before driving back; he allowed himself an exit in the "Action."

Travel plans were worked on:

JOSEF: Don't you wish we could somehow get there faster? Without the hassle of planes and the problems with driving?

MARCEL: Everything's so very expensive.

JOSEF: Carpooling?

MARCEL: Unrealistic.

JOSEF: Whose car do we take?

MARCEL: We'll worry about that later.

JOSEF: That's the most important part of the Action.

MARCEL: My Father's one friend has a Piper Cub and could give us a lift.

JOSEF: To all these places we want to go? Not likely.

MARCEL: That's what I thought. So flying is out, the trains are gone, the skywalk is gone and we're left with primitive cars. Better than nothing, I suppose.

9.

The ideas everyone had regarding the Action/Event were debated rigorously for a period of a couple of weeks; to solidify them, they all agreed to gather for a very gaudy, expensive final meal in town. Everyone had decided to go with posh fusion and get exotic sushi and mushrooms and beer at Murasame's, the location picked by Amelia and booked by Cameron. The atmosphere was congested but the ambience was warm - the prices were, as expected, completely outrageous but for the last meal spent it was considered "worth it." The restaurant's visuals were impressive: monitors of all shapes and sizes peered out from every wall, filled with gorgeous stop-motion imagery of flowers blossoming and clips from black and white cinema (sound nonexistent) or rare foreign animated treasures, like Svankmajer's *Darkness/Light/Darkness* and Wladyslaw Starewicz's *The Mascot* playing in loops, and those were just the ones that a stunned and preoccupied Josef could identify as he was twirling his head around to examine them all. The flat television at their horseshoe-shaped booth had a mélange of different channels to choose from, but none of them carried the films Josef was gawking at - instead, the pictures were from cameras placed high above the other booths and tables in the restaurant, in the kitchen (you could watch as the food was being prepared), behind the bar where drinks were being mixed, at the hostess' pavilion and even outside, into the narrow, bustling street. The idea of watching people all around you from your own private enclave was a perverse pleasure - and Warholian in its passive/intrusive gaze. Everyone at the table thought the design ingenious.

While they were enjoying their Hoegaarden and picking at the bread assortment brought to them on a rotating, three-tiered display stand, all addressed problems they had with the trip. Cameron, who was more for the idea than anyone would have imagined, posed (expectedly) the most questions, namely regarding payment, items needed to travel with and such, which were good for the group because Marcel, Amelia and Josef were not really planning it all that well in their minds. Amelia talked about her most recent conversation with Naomi and her thoughts on bringing with her several (actually, two) people with her to stay as well - Cameron remarked how awkward the conversation must have been, but Amelia said Naomi was amused by the idea of housing a whole Troupe/Commune with her and that, conveniently, she had enough room. Naomi, Josef remarked, could be something of an Aldous Huxleyesque cult revivalist, and she might have liked the idea of their Action.

They discussed the finer and finer points of the matter well into the night, as they walked and talked. Josef was pleased he was getting a ride down to Louisiana, and that was really all he cared about. He offered advice and contributed to the Dialogue when necessary, but was more consumed with his own anxiety regarding going back to class, doing the work-due-tomorrow grind, wondering how the town would treat him and how he would react to the town. "The voodoo of the location is vital," he thought to himself.

At 1:30 in the morning, around the time everyone has to find their way to their cars, into cabs and back in their own homes, or in the homes of others, Cameron felt queasy and needed antacids, Amelia was drained of energy and Marcel was in a land of his own, concocting a plan he was going to spring on everyone at the last minute because that was the way Marcel was and that was what he wanted to do. When Josef found himself back in his own place, he turned on the coffee pot in the kitchen and dug wine crackers out of the cupboards and turned on a bootleg of Lee Strasburg on video cassette - the tape roughshod and shaky - conducting one of his seminars. He was talking in a fury, and moving, and pointing, all to a very interested, very enraptured crowd, who hung onto his every word. Cameron asked for a copy when Josef was done, and after Cameron was through with it Marcel wanted it. Josef could have gone to bed, but was buzzing and alert - alcohol, he found, made him hyper instead of lethargic.

Marcel did not plan to tell his parents what was going to happen, what his ideas were, not because he disliked them, but because he felt like he was helping them rid themselves of him, of unburdening their house for a period of time with his presence. He had been, for the past several/couple/few years, orderly, calm, collected and reasonable and the move was designed to be instant, painless and unorthodox. It was never a decision made out of spite, like when husbands abruptly leave their families because they despise them. He particularly liked the impromptu drive out West because many of the great, great figures of history were unorthodox, and he wanted to be unorthodox. Except for Kant. Kant was orthodox.

He didn't know what to tell Lucile, how to explain to her his temporary/permanent leave, how to keep her from hating him. He did not know if she hated him before, if she would hate him for his immediate departure, or what she would say if he told her to keep everything a secret. She would, no doubt, have many questions. Could she be trusted? Marcel saw himself as being non-confrontational, non-explicit, non-personal: it was the best route he could foresee in this matter. Some may have interpreted it as cowardly, but the non-committal stance is effective - no words needed to be exchanged, and yet everything is said by action.

He lollygagged through the two weeks of preparation for the trip, and mentally parsed out the things that needed to be accomplished in the meantime. He had his game plan, and frequently met with the members of the Troupe at the Kashmir Tea Bar for quiet, relaxation (the Bar was nothing but couches, coffee tables and small wooden pillars for you to set your clear glasses of heavily-sweetened green tea on or small dessert or bowl of soup on). Josef spent a decent amount of time in there sampling the assortment of teas and got everyone else addicted by using it as a casual, mid-afternoon conversational meet-and-greet. You could actually sit there, and *talk*. No loud music as in bars or clubs or in bar-clubs for you to scream over, for you to be sickened by, just a conversational lounge. When he and Cameron and Marcel met one day at noon, Cameron and Josef were waiting for Marcel, and questioned why Marcel didn't discuss the trip with Marcel's family, queried as to why last minute changes were being made spontaneously and various other points of purpose and reference. Marcel had some things to bring up to them, too - things they did not expect:

CAMERON: Let me get this straight: we're all going in a tractor-trailer?

JOSEF: There will be four of us in there for a good deal of time. *Four*.

MARCEL: (*Pause*) It's an extra wide cabin and it's a single seat - it will be compressed a little but I think it would work out.

CAMERON: Amelia's going to object.

MARCEL: If she has something better to add, hey, let's go with that.

JOSEF: (*Shakes head*) Where did you come up with this?

MARCEL: (*Pause*) My Father needs me to take a large shipment of salmon all the way out there. I said I wanted to do it. He said he didn't want me to. I said I have to. While I was going, I told him I was bringing people along with me to drop off along the way. His company pays for the gas, and everyone has a mode of transportation, and the order is delivered. In fact, all of you would be doing me a big favor by going with me and helping me out.

JOSEF: It's going to be uncomfortable.

CAMERON: (*Incredulous*) They don't have salmon on the West Coast?

JOSEF: (*Puzzled*) I thought that was delivered long distances by other means.

MARCEL: I just do as I'm told.

CAMERON: Planes won't do it?

JOSEF: Expensive.

CAMERON: (*Pause. Scratches face.*) Trains?

JOSEF: Don't get me going on trains now.

CAMERON: We know, don't start.

The truth was, Marcel did not have to make a delivery, but his stone-faced delivery suggested otherwise. He felt his idea was the most original and efficient, if not the most comfortable, and was driven to have others see it his way. The tractor-trailer would indeed be cramped, but it would also be personal, and in being personal, more memorable. He also saw the advantage to having the tractor-trailer *in that* he wouldn't have to pay for the gas and wouldn't simply glide down the highway, tiny and impersonal, but roar and rage and be noticed.

10.

Amelia was not briefed until the last minute about the confined space in the tractor-trailer, but by the time she was told it could hardly matter to her, bored and determined as she was to gain in experience and avoid emotional and professional stagnation - nonsense fun, nonsense fun. She was a little concerned about how successful the voyage would be, but felt it had to be better than where she was at, since where you are is never where you want to be, always needing to go elsewhere, and so you strive for elsewhere and hope for it to be everything you dreamed it could be. Frisco is not the Frisco-Frisco it was anymore, but it's still standing and that's what is important. The Frisco-Frisco is a myth, as are any other cornerstones of the past that were once heralded as being shining and relevant; symbolic empires do not last forever (the Ottoman Empire did not last forever, the Roman Empire did not last forever and the American Empire will not last forever). Her parents thought it foolish but sanctioned her release; she expected more hostility but they were so preoccupied with her Father's job security - as a welder - that any good news from her, for once, would be a blessing.

Marcel agreed to handle the traveling directions, and sought the assistance of the Philadelphia Motor and Travel Bureau, where his parents were members, to plan the itinerary. Using their computers they printed out a Travel Booklet for him - perfectly bound and with a matte cover - that detailed every stretch of their prospective route from Pennsylvania to New Orleans to Santa Fe to San Diego along the coast to San Francisco - the Booklet, crammed with mini-maps and sickeningly precise directions, predicted that the trip would take over 57 hours to complete, and that was, apparently, if they were driving straight through. He thanked the ladies that put it together - a bunch of neo-hippie old women, pleasant and calm and prone to saying things like, "Settle down, you're too jumpy," and "Oh! _____ [specific location] is so pretty! I went there back in..." They asked him for his destination points - or points of interest - and the entire project was typed, printed and justified in evenly rowed boxes of text and symbols. There was no rush to get the entire trip finished in all fifty-plus hours, so that predicted number was immediately disregarded.

Marcel spoke with Amelia and Cameron about objects to bring, and the topic of money came up once more. They all brought an assortment of credit cards and wallets (and a purse) with a certain amount of cash needed. The proper transfer of funds from the East Coast to the West Coast would come much later. Long-term details were to be handled later. When needed.

Large-scale collectibles and furniture had to be sacrificed for the time being - things like books and paperwork and trinkets were boxed and to be shipped. Clothes not needed for the trip would also be sent later. Personal items required for the trip - undergarments, toiletries - were packed up in suitcases and then the suitcases were placed in plastic bags to keep the smell from the trailer end of the tractor from infecting them. A minimal amount of items were put in the front due to space constraints. Small personal bags were placed in the sleeping cabin. Snacks and bottles of water were stored in there as well. Josef's friend Terrence headed down to New Orleans a week earlier in his Father's pickup truck and took almost all of Josef's belongings already, and given Josef's lack of interest in loading and unloading anything heavy, only the smallest and lightest objects were taken - namely, two tiny dressers and a half-sized desk. Easy in, easy out, nothing should be heavy enough to make an impression in the carpet; nothing should be too large to have to dust frequently.

Marcel set his radio alarm very early the day of departure to ensure that he had taken all precautions and also packed his vitals in the bag containing his deodorant, cologne and objects used to clean and preserve his teeth. It occurred to him that he would need a physician's approval to continue refilling his prescription vials, though he quickly dismissed that small quirk as something to wrestle with later. He rehearsed the lines he was going to give everyone in the Troupe in case they pressured him with elaborate questions, although he anticipated that nothing would be said to him at all, and only the most cursory of answers was needed at the ready.

He went into Lucile's bedroom and looked at her for one last time - he set his hand on the tussled brunette locks briefly before slowly creeping back outside. Outside his parents' bedroom door, he didn't dare fiddle with the doorknob, and kissed his palm and gently placed it against the wooden wall. He took his car keys and packed belongings and bolted out of the house and tore through the road: he was running late and wanted to get a nice start to the day - the sky had not yet become its almost transparent blue and the majority of his city was first becoming conscious.

Marcel had to use his key to get the tractor-trailer at his Father's Headquarters since none of the people that worked there (especially secretary Sally) were not going to be there and the place was mercifully vacant - it made it much easier for him to get in, load up the rear of the tractor-trailer with the cartons of fish and head off. Hauling the cartons was understandably difficult and heavy, and he was in a gigantic hurry, making the picking up and carrying that much more of a challenge. Normally that was not *really* his job - others basically handled unloading and loading -

and taking things manually and individually was a pressing problem. Marcel had no time to think about the struggle, and walked the cases inside of the refrigerated storage area and scrambled to get the next batch.

It took him an hour-and-a-half of labor to fill the back ¾ of the way full, and afterwards ran to the showers and rinsed himself off. The time read 5:40, and he was pressed to gather his friends and get rambling. He picked up Amelia first, who was pacing and ready and Josef second, who was bringing out filled cartons with novels, essays and folders with loose papers in them.

JOSEF: Will these fit back there?

MARCEL: I thought I told you to give that stuff to Terrence!

JOSEF: So you can't fit three small boxes in the back?

MARCEL: (*Rolls eyes*) I guess.

Cameron was the last to gather, and also the hardest to round up - his house rested smack in the middle of a very narrow street, and he was not waiting outside with his meager belongings as was stipulated in their Pre-Action Planning. He had his silk pajamas on and was in his green house slippers, but his bags were packed, thank heaven.

CAMERON: I had problems sleeping and now I'm having trouble waking up to us.

Amelia, un-amused, hustled him out of there, grabbing two of his bags (Josef and Marcel lent minor assistance) and pushed him into his bedroom so he could finally get dressed. He stumbled out of his room several minutes later, informed everyone they needed to cease rushing him, then ran to the kitchen, snagged a handful of English Breakfast tea bags ("Oh, I need those"), wedged them into his shorts pocket and like a Romeroesque zombie, lurched towards the tractor-trailer ("That's a fucking huge ride"). Josef suggested that he sleep in the cabin for the first stretch to get his wits about him and lose the sea legs he was sporting … and liking the idea so much, he took them up on it.

CAMERON: I watched a show on the Food Network that showed you what wines you drink with what meals - I can never remember - and then got caught up reading some bogus article in *Rolling Stone* on how managers have notoriously mistreated their talent over the last fifty-odd years. (*Pause*) I just couldn't sleep. I'm always like that. I get tired and hyper the night before Christmas and my birthday, too.

The Troupe, armed with their key belongings and no more, set out. Marcel, who would have to bear the brunt of driving the entire trip, declared that he needed, at all times, one person to stay awake with him and act as his navigator and keep tabs in their Custom Travel Booklet as to where they were at all times. Amelia volunteered to be navigator at first because she was the most awake, while Josef, at the far right, slouched downwards into his seat and settled in. She took the book, flipped through several pages, and began uttering, aloud, the roads he needed to take out of Philadelphia. As she spoke, Josef started thinking, and as he started thinking, he became paranoid.

JOSEF: Do you have that card to pay for the gas?

MARCEL: Yes, I have the gas card.

JOSEF: (*Shakes head*) Ah.

(*Pause*)

JOSEF: Do you have to go to those weigh stations along the side of the highway?

MARCEL: If they're open, yes.

JOSEF: (*Pause*) How long will that take?

MARCEL: (*Thinking*) I couldn't tell you. Not that long, I hope.

(*Pause*)

JOSEF: So, when does this fish shipment have to be delivered by?

MARCEL: Let me worry about that.

JOSEF: (*Pause*) But it has to be by a certain time?

MARCEL: It'll get there.

JOSEF: It won't rot?

(*Amelia turns to Josef and smiles shrewdly.*)

MARCEL: You were back there. It's cool.

JOSEF: I mean, even *with* the cool temperatures, won't they get old? Stale?

MARCEL: …

JOSEF: I'm just making sure.

AMELIA: (*Interrupting*) I think you need to make the exit coming up next.

JOSEF: I have to tell you, it's neat being this high and looking down on the cars. (*He sits up in his seat*) I can't see their faces - I can only make out legs and hands, but the feeling being this high over them is … really something.

11.

The first forty-five minutes of driving for them were quiet - morning fatigue was still covering the three in the front like plaque, and the initial adjustment to the move was first settling in. The fear of change was there, the fear of failure was there, the fear of disaster was there. All looked along the highway and across the glistening, painted metal machines and the somnambulant commuters operating them, and wondered where they were headed, what they were doing and what they were listening to.

After the quiet period ended, they began discussing the road itinerary, when to stop and eat, and approximately where they would bed down. Josef, out of the blue, took out a knife and made an inscription into the dash of the tractor-trailer. It looked like:

AMELIA: Is that an "R?"

JOSEF: Cameron told me to do it. He said it's the rune for good travel.

MARCEL: You just carved into my Father's tractor-trailer.

JOSEF: It's good luck.

MARCEL: Hm. (*Pause*) The thought's there.

JOSEF: And it's not that large, either.

AMELIA: (*Turning to face Josef*) I didn't know you were superstitious.

JOSEF: I'm not. I think Cameron is. (*Pause*) Where are we now?

They tried to decide which state they should stop at for lunch. (Matters like this were considered set and decided a period of time ago, during the discussion and planning stages, but those plans were either mentally dismembered or misplaced in the interim.) It was ruled, in the front of the tractor-trailer (without Cameron's vote) that unless there was an emergency, bathroom breaks would be taken when more than one person insisted.

The vehicle had no audio equipment, television monitors or computer jacks in it - there was nothing stimulating to keep everyone rapt with attention. Amelia proposed that they start by telling stories - Marcel responded that the stories would grow tiring immediately. Josef inquired as to what kind of stories they should tell, and Amelia responded that they should be invented, to stir the mind and encourage creativity.

MARCEL: I'm not that creative.

AMELIA: Then we should tell stories about ourselves.

JOSEF: Personal stories?

AMELIA: Stories from before. Stories that changed you. Implanted themselves inside of your head.

JOSEF: Subject matter-wise, what were you thinking of?

MARCEL: Isn't this like a middle school sleepover and all of us take turns and gush over who we think is cute?

AMELIA: No. I'm suggesting we tell stories that no one else knows. About things that we would never want anyone else to know. Or things that trouble you. Stories, ideas. Like that.

JOSEF: Like the first person I kissed?

MARCEL: Oh, this is truth or dare.

AMELIA: It's not truth or dare at all. There is no dare. You tell what stories you want to tell, and not tell the ones you're not comfortable in telling. It's story hour.

MARCEL: And they have to be true?

AMELIA: They should be true. If you lie and you're good we might never know. But that's cheating. You should tell the story as you saw it happen.

JOSEF: (*Pause*) Things that bother us?

AMELIA: Of course.

JOSEF: How personal?

AMELIA: Personal.

MARCEL: I'm not sure what this is supposed to do.

AMELIA: It's a way of revealing yourself one layer at a time. It's a method of getting to know what goes through our heads, collectively.

JOSEF: (*Sighs*) It's too early for this.

MARCEL: I get it. We start the narrative *now*, at the beginning, introduce the characters as best as possible, set the scene, roll out the story and end it appropriately.

JOSEF: Ah! So it can have a beginning, middle and end, but not necessarily in that order.

AMELIA: Sure, but ... shouldn't it be told in a straightforward manner?

(*Extended pause*)

MARCEL: Okay, so how do we start this?

AMELIA: We start at the beginning.

MARCEL: Who starts?

THE 4ᵀᴴ GRADE

AMELIA: We rode to school and back on the same bus - he lived right down the block from me. Michael. I remember him transferring over to our school in second grade, but he was in the other homeroom. I would see him and the other boys play Four-Square - this bouncing ball game that's a lot like dodge ball - in the recess yard and my friends and I wanted to play, too, but the boys always yelled at us for trying to join so we stayed away.

When we went to third grade, he had a birthday party and invited everyone from both classes. It was held in his family's basement. I went, and my Mom drove my friend Aimee - who later transferred to another school - and we were the only two girls at the party. I brought him, as a gift, a spaceship that you put in your bathtub (it's like a rubber duck but gray) that had star-shaped soaps stuck to the side of it. I know, my Mom bought it for me to give to him. What was I supposed to get? I think Aimee's parents gave her - to give to him - a gift certificate to go bowling.

But at the party, he hardly talked to us. Aimee and I talked to each other, or just sat there while everyone else ran around. Michael's Father put the original *Wizard of Oz* on and we all watched that, and eventually my Mom came back and picked us up. When we were leaving his parents told him to say "goodbye" to us, but he didn't, and we got the feeling he and his friends didn't want us there, or were laughing at us.

So we went back to school, and nobody talked about the party. I was really saddened by the whole thing. In a week or so, our teacher, who was very young - God, she must have been our age then - moved our seats around, and who did she sit next to me but Michael. He was quiet and didn't say anything, and I recall being really mad, so I didn't want to sit by him. But then it came to reading time, and he saw that I had *The Voyages of Doctor Dolittle*. He told me he loved that book. When I told him I liked it, he became interested, talking about how much he liked, oh, the characters and the monkey Chee-Chee - about how much he read. The next day he brought in a copy of *The Little Prince* and told me to keep it. I said I didn't want it, that he should keep it, but he told me he had three copies.

On the bus ride home - it was on a Friday, too - he sat next to me. Aimee usually sat there, but she had to be picked up by her Mom for whatever reason straight from school. Just as we were sitting there, and in between him talking about books, he leaned over and kissed me on the cheek. Just like that. I was shocked, and rubbed my face with my hand. I think he was shocked too, and got out of his seat and ran to the back of the bus with his friends. I didn't get up and turn around because I was afraid they were laughing at me or at him, I'm not sure, but I didn't move. His bus stop came first, and I didn't even notice him walk past me down the center aisle of the bus. All I saw was Michael step out of the bus, onto the sidewalk, and run down the block. The bus lurched forward and I didn't see where he was going - he was in mid-stride before the trees blocked my view of him. I don't remember if I told my Mom when I got home or not, but I do remember that I wanted to wash my face.

JOSEF: What happened the next Monday? Did you say anything?
AMELIA: Nothing was said. That just happened. We did keep talking about books, though - so that didn't stop - but he was such a rambling loudmouth that our teacher moved us apart because we were too disruptive to the class. I had

a crush on someone else after that, I think, so it didn't matter.

JOSEF: (*Beaming*) At nine you were already a failure at love.

MARCEL: Is that really true? Or maybe I heard someone else tell something similar.

AMELIA: I think it's every girl's first story.

MARCEL: You're speaking for them?

AMELIA: I'm giving my own account. (*Pause*) I'm positive I'm not alone.

One thing that was apparent to those riding alongside Marcel, and Marcel alongside them, was how profoundly monotonous the road seemed. Parallel to the road on both sides were purposely-planted tree lines, blocking the view of the environment beyond the asphalt and the cars and trucks. Josef, staring out his side window, let his focus give way, and visually registered the endlessly green textures run from right to left as if it were an endless whip-pan, or maybe even a hand-painted film by Brakhage on the clear slide that was the tractor-trailer window. Occasionally, along hilly parts of the road, mountains or hills or different landmasses could be seen interrupting the flow of greenery. But other than the foliage and the sun's reflection off the other cars and the grassy strip dividing the to-and-fro flow of the road, there was nothing much to see. But, they thought, it was only the first fraction of their trip, and perhaps the topography would alter itself.

To continue their storytelling venture, Marcel added to Amelia's story with some thoughts of his own. It had been quiet in the car and everyone was content to just sit and observe. All were wondering how Cameron was doing in the sleeping cabin, and Marcel was keeping an eye on the road and on the fuel gauge.

MARCEL: What I find so interesting about Amelia's story is how I never had an experience like that when I was in grade school. I don't remember grade school, because I didn't stay in any one place long enough to know anyone. Every time I went into a new class, I found myself trying to make adjustments all over. It was different, and difficult. It took me a long time to develop a crush on someone, and I find that for me to even want to be with someone, I have to really know something personal about them.

JOSEF: I get what you're saying - I don't like the idea of the one-night stand myself, it's too defeating and impersonal and sad. Let me just say this:

THE 6TH GRADE

JOSEF: Picking up where Amelia stopped, I had this crush, too, and it was in the sixth grade. I don't know what in particular I liked about this girl, which is strange trying to remember it now, but it just happened to me. You don't know at 11 or 12 why you like someone. You just do. You also don't know what you want from them. You can't take them out on dates - neither of you can drive or have money. It's goofy if you think about it ... there's really no direct point. It's an initiation that your body springs on you early on to be honed and developed to form later relationships.

Anyway, my affection at the time was reserved for a strange girl named Sonia who everyone called Liz. I don't remember why. I tried to hide that I liked her - I never told my friends or spoke about her, but she figured it out, somehow. Well, we were both invited to a Halloween party by my friend Pat, who had it at his house. After 4 PM my Mom dropped me off. I was dressed up, and this is the kicker, like Cary Grant.

AMELIA: (*Interrupting*) Get out! That young?

JOSEF: It's true! I had a tuxedo, a top hat, my hair combed just right, I even tried to do his voice. "Dry your eyes, baby, it's out of character." I used to watch his movies, even very young, with my Grandmother, who had them on all day, and her and I came up with the idea for the costume. To help out, my Dad came up with the idea to put an enlarged photocopy of Grant's face on a piece of cardboard that he attached to a wooden stick for me to put up to my own face.

AMELIA: (*Interrupting*) You were a weird kid.

JOSEF: So, I go to a party like this, and Sonia is there, and she's dolled up like Gene Simmons from KISS, with the face paint and KISS t-shirt.

MARCEL: (*Interrupting*) No armor?

JOSEF: No, no armor. (*Resuming story*) But I saw her, and her friend, who I was in a Reading Group with at the time - (*Pause*) and I can't recall her name for the life of me - and I got in the moment and said to Sonia, "Hey KISS." Both of them, her and her friend, turned to look at me, and Sonia said, "I'm Gene Simmons." I tried to explain my costume to them and they didn't get it, but they said they liked it.

Later, we were all waiting outside for our parents to pick us up and I was trying to talk to her about KISS, since I didn't know much about the group. Hell, I still don't care. But her Father, parked down the street, came up to us and told her he was waiting for her. He looked at me before he and Sonia left, and he asked me what my "get-up" was all about. I told him - I figured he would know. He said, "Yeah, yeah" and that was that.

But weeks later, one of the parents called up my Mom and told her that Sonia's Father called one or two of the other parents to tell them that I was a "fag" and "a poison" and that I shouldn't be invited to anyone else's parties or anything like that. I didn't know what that meant, exactly - I had an idea - and it was the first time my parents and I had a sit-down to talk about what he said. I was horrified and embarrassed because my parents looked embarrassed. Unfortunately, this resentment bled into my dealing with her in school - it wasn't her fault, but I blamed her, which I shouldn't have. When you're young, I think, you aren't sure what's going on and you just react. You get lost in it all, and are so desperate to get older and discover the truth. When you're an adult, you then want to go back to childhood, with what you've learned, and make it all right again.

The incident did do one small thing for me: it was the last costume party I ever attended.

12.

They enjoyed lunch at 1:30 PM in the state of Virginia - Josef wanted to eat light because he knew his stomach couldn't handle too much, and Amelia wanted something quick and cheap. They settled at a quiet diner that was packed with cars - Marcel took great caution to park as far away from the other vehicles as possible. They awoke Cameron from his munificent slumber - by banging loudly on the cabin door - and he appeared, initially, pale and sickly, but his attitude was jubilant and he claimed to be ready to eat. He swore not to sleep in the back quarters again, claiming that the tight quarters sleeping and bumpiness were not at all pleasant.

CAMERON: It would not alarm me to know that truck drivers were heavily into sleeping medication and not-sleeping medication: sometimes the body and mind must be whipped into formless submission.

All four were seated in a non-smoking booth in the corner where they rolled their necks, rubbed their faces and cursed the glaring sunshine but were grateful for no rain. Amelia assured Cameron that they'd always be there when he awoke; he nodded and expressed gratitude. All four ordered regular coffee; Marcel mulled over places to visit in his Custom Travel Booklet before they arrived in New Orleans and tried to set a time frame for how long they should spend there and Josef brought Cameron up to speed on what Oral Project they started to take them through the trip.

CAMERON: So it's like we're at camp and these are bedtime stories.

AMELIA: Were you ever at camp?

CAMERON: No.

AMELIA: Good, because it's nothing like that.

Amelia and Josef enlightened him to the finer points of the stories told, that they had already started at the beginning and have been steadily moving forward, and that honesty was neither rewarded nor condemned, that the story should be 'sold' by the teller and 'bought' by the recipient.

JOSEF: If you wish to contribute, you must contribute in the proper place.

AMELIA: The order is very important.

Cameron was hesitant to participate, feeding everyone with lines about 'not having anything valid to offer,' and about how 'happy men have no stories,' but it was obvious that he wasn't exactly sure of the directions and that they would have to be recited, once more, for his benefit. After the second explanation, he agreed with them that it's an exquisite idea and that he would pick and choose his moments to chime in.

Before all four left the diner, they took turns to use the lavatories and wash up. They each paid for their respective meals and collectively added a 15% tip at the behest of Amelia, who felt pity for the middle-aged waitress who brought the food, was under appreciated, and had to work at a no-name diner in nowhere Virginia.

Outside, they loaded into the tractor-trailer and immediately felt the squeeze of the third man inside. All of them were now cramped and shoulder-to-shoulder and skin to skin, and that was the way it was simply going to have to be. Josef volunteered to stay in the cabin in the back, but his peers 'knew him' and knew of his anxiety regarding tight spaces; Amelia said she would go back 'if she had to' but no one was forcing her.

MARCEL: We knew it was going to be like this from the beginning.

Before the tractor-trailer drove out of the lot, Josef on the far left and Marcel on the far right cracked open their windows ¼ of the way, to try to circulate the recycled air.

After several miles were behind him, Cameron spoke up:

THE NUMBER ONE FIASCO

CAMERON: Amelia knows about this, but I'm not sure you guys do, so I have to tell you about this girl none of you ever met named Angelica. She was the most aggressive girl I'd ever met. She was a cheerleader - fit, attractive, long legs, kinky, mixed-tone hair, dimples - but not exactly *popular*: whenever I mentioned her to some of the guys in our class, they looked at me crooked and didn't know where I was coming from. Well, aside from cheerleading, she was also in Drama Club, which I was planning to be in, but never went and joined because I didn't want to look like a fool in front of her. In fact, I realized that whenever I find myself really attracted to someone, I immediately turn to spin control and do whatever I can to avoid her or say bad things about her behind her back. I'd rather have someone think I hate her than like her since that way she can never respond negatively back to me.

So with Angelica, it was the same way. I kept a makeshift diary during high school which I still have - in fact, Amelia's looked at it a couple of times. I think we read it one night over coffee and pie. I was petrified of anyone ever finding it, but it was too personal for me to just throw away. As a matter of fact, I was so paranoid, I never wrote her name in the book: I always referred to her as #1, just to keep it simple. At the time, I had a few friends who knew, and to them I called her #1.

I'm not sure around what time it started happening, but in Civics class she sat next to me - we had those individual desks that were in rows - and she always sat in her chair sideways, looking directly at me. We also had Calculus together, and since, again, we were permitted to choose our own seats, she planted herself directly next to me. Her presence took over my concentration. I didn't know what to say to her. At one point, we had a study period in class and we had to do group work and she actually put her feet right on the side of my seat, exposing her bare legs and watching me through shaded eyes. No one paid attention to her, but I found the experience to be irritating - she was challenging me to react, and I didn't. I had to play my character straight, and pretended her face was a rolling camera I was not supposed to look into. It became a test: endure the class, retain composure, ignore the things that needed to be ignored.

At lunch one day, one of her few friends sat at our table. She told me she needed to speak to me, and "politely informed me" that Angelica liked me. You know what I said? "Oh, that's nice." That's it. My cover had been blown - my internal intent was hidden. Like Sontag said of Barthes, his interest in you tended to be equal to your interest in him. It's the same thing here - maybe she felt that I was interested in her, or some prescient gadfly told her so, and that's why she became interested in me. Maybe my avoiding her and rolling my eyes when her name was mentioned wasn't so convincing. The whole thing rattled me, because I didn't know what to do next. Would I go out to dinner with her? Did she like movies? What if I did something wrong? If I went into class the next Monday, would the story of what I did wrong leak through the school? Would she betray me?

It was fitting, too, that during Graduation, for our classes' procession into the auditorium, I was paired up with her to walk down the aisle - the selection was according to height, I think. In fact, while walking, and amidst the paparazzi parents with their flash bulbs and slow-motion faces, she turned and said something to me, and since I didn't hear her - the music was loud - I didn't say anything in response. I nodded but never turned to look at her face.

I believe she said to me, "This is going to last all night," but to this day I'm still not sure.

13.

By the time they stopped to eat dinner, they'd gone through two Weigh Stations - where they waited for a very long time in very long lines - and three spontaneous storms that dumped a deluge of rainwater on top of the tractor-trailer and slowed down traffic to an absolute crawl - the mist and fog made Marcel squint and lean forward in his seat while his three co-pilots alerted him to this or that on the road - busted tires in the middle of the lane, almost invisible motorcyclists swerving between everyone, cars mysteriously braking and/or stopping. They ate outside Knoxville at another small diner Josef spotted. They needed fuel, and that, too, was at the exit stop.

After ordering and receiving their four cups of regular coffee, Amelia spoke:

THE FRIENDS OF AMELIA'S YOUTH

AMELIA: Marcel, do you happen to remember Regine?
MARCEL: Absolutely.
JOSEF: (*Chuckles*) I do.

AMELIA: She was having trouble at home - I don't know if you knew, but her Father abused her and her Mother, her Mother didn't have much time for her or her Brother, so she spent a lot of time at my house and we played basketball together and watched television and went for bike rides. Her and I were close. So, you know her Father did leave her family in a storm when she was thirteen, and her

Mom had to do the job of raising them, and she was in a financial strain to keep up payments on the cars and private school. So Regine really tried to help out at home and do whatever she needed - she helped her Brother with his homework and cleaned the house and made dinner for her Mom when she was working two jobs.

Now, I'm not sure what prompted this, but we were both 14 or 15, she and I were walking around the block - it was a nice day and we didn't have any plans - and she starts asking about what I think about Brooke, who's in class with us. Do I ever talk to her? What's she like? Brooke and I were on the JV Basketball squad together, but aside from that I couldn't say. That's all she talked about, what classes she had with Brooke and what classes I had with Brooke … it never fazed me why she wanted to know - I never thought much of Brooke, though I admit I barely knew her except that she slacked off in practice and was always badmouthing someone else, although thinking back we all did that in one way or another. So then she started coming with me to practice so she could talk to Brooke. After that, it was Brooke, Regine and myself playing basketball, hanging out, and just doing nothing together. The three of us got along well for a couple weeks despite my initial displeasure with Brooke's presence.

But then a little after that, Regine stopped returning my phone calls, saying she was "busy" and her and Brooke spent a lot of time without me. I wasn't mad, but it really bothered me. At school, there were rumors about the two of them that I caught wind of, stuff I didn't know was true or not. I gathered a lot of people didn't really like Brooke, and suspected her - and now Regine - of things I couldn't prove and didn't believe. The guys in class avoided both of them, and since I was going out with Jesse at the time, I had him tell me what he heard. He didn't want to get involved in it - he liked Regine, I think - and said he didn't know, but she was my friend and I was obligated to stand up for her.

When I talked to both Brooke and Regine about what I heard, they wanted to know what was being said. Well, I told them that I heard they were doing cocaine in the cemetery after school, that they were going to parties at the local colleges, that Brooke and her Brother were involved in selling drugs, that Brooke was involved with a married man and other rumors of virulent intent, they became upset with me. They both vehemently denied any and all charges, and were so mad I brought it up in front of them they didn't talk to me for weeks. I tried to explain to them that I was just telling them what everyone else was saying - and that I was defending them. Neither saw it that way.

The rumors didn't stop, and I tried to stay neutral, but we were never the same since. About a year later, around Prom Time, they decided they were going to go to the Prom with each other. I tried to tell them that since it was a private school, they were not allowed to go with each other - they each had to have a date of the opposite sex. They claimed it meant nothing, that they just wanted to go to the Prom, but the Prom Committee did not understand and refused. To help them, I concocted a little plan: I personally sought out dates for them.

Jesse's friends were all taken, so after some looking around I found two guys that didn't have anyone to go with - Kevin and Jeremy that I had English class with. I ran it by them, I ran it by Regine and Brooke, everyone reluctantly agreed, and I had considered myself a matchmaker.

Prom Night, all of us sat together at the same table, but the evening was far from quick. Both Regine and Brooke showed up slightly tipsy and after twenty minutes into the night, they disappeared into the bathroom. They were seated with us one minute, and then completely gone the next. They abandoned Kevin and Jeremy, who were embarrassed and befuddled. Regine and Brooke, who wanted to be the talk of the Prom, willed themselves to be the talk of the Prom by making a scene. But most of all, I felt like they were getting even with me for setting it up, and I felt like I was responsible for Kevin and Jeremy's situation.

The two of them went to school days later and acted like nothing had happened, which further alienated them from the rest of the school. In strangely justifiable fashion, however, Brooke's Brother was arrested two years later for cocaine possession and reckless driving, and put in jail. I have no idea what happened to Brooke, but Regine left town with her Mother. Last we spoke, she said she was engaged, but I was not invited to any of the festivities.

14.

Fatigue set in completely - making cowards of them all - and Marcel, who had gotten up earlier than everyone else in the morning, wanted to find a hotel as soon as possible. They found a Motel 8 in Birmingham and got a single, two-bed room for $40, which was to be split four ways. Everyone was comfortable with the decision to stop and end the day. Amelia got her own bed, Marcel and Josef set their pride aside and shared the second bed and Cameron volunteered to sleep in the room chair since he said he could "sleep anywhere." The bathroom door had a massive crack in it and the sink's hot water did not work - the bed shared by Marcel and Josef had football-sized blood stains along the outer edge that dripped onto the light brown carpet. When Cameron got a towel from the bathroom to cover it with, the blood seeped through. Everyone was so fatigued that they turned off the lights and pretended not to notice.

In the middle of the night, Cameron awoke suddenly, eyes wide open and light-headed. He reassembled the still images from his memory into a semi-narrative:

THE DREAM OF HALLWAYS

CAMERON: I was walking down the hall of a cruise ship, and there were thousands of doors running up and down the hallway, and through the one door emerged this strobing light that went down the hallway - it was like a floating orb that was too bright to look at but shined over everything within thirty feet of it. I followed it down to the end of the hallway, where I walked into it and stepped into a spacious dance hall where people were in tuxedos and slow-stepped with one another. In the middle of the room was a swimming pool where two nude girls did laps - back and forth, back and forth. I approached some woman to dance with but she declined, saying that the sores on my skin were an abomination. So, panicked, I ran past the pianist and the hors d'oeuvre trays and the jammed-full bar area into another place filled with mousetraps that I carefully stepped around. I looked and looked, but I could only find a Women's Bathroom. When I went in, there were no toilets, only mirrors, and the mirrors were on the ceilings, the floors, the walls ... and through all of them I could see my skin distended, my face deformed and bloated, my teeth cracked and broken and my hands and ankles covered with purple lumps.

I was so panicked, I shook uncontrollably, and that was when the sequence ended.

15.

Josef was going to take a stab at what Cameron's dream meant, but decided against it, particularly because his scrambled eggs and Tabasco arrived in front of him in due time and he lost the will to decipher the mess. Amelia looked frazzled, with her hair soaked and stringy and the mauve t-shirt she wore pressed firmly against her skin. Cameron and Marcel tried not to look at her.

Amelia calculated that they would be in New Orleans by 5 PM or so, and suggested that Josef call Terrence an hour or two before their ETA to make sure he was in his apartment and/or available to give directions. Marcel's Custom Travel Booklet was reliable up to a point, but its maps did not include absolutely every single street and alleyway, and where they could safely leave the tractor-trailer for the duration of their stay there. That was a matter to which Terrence could provide adequate assistance.

After breakfast and in the tractor-trailer, Amelia goaded Josef into relaying some personal information in a timely fashion keeping with the Rules that had been stipulated and making sure his personal information kept consistent with the running narrative's timeline. As Josef spoke, the sky turned gray and dense, forbidding the light from the sun to pour through trembling holes and onto the matter below and constantly threatening of rain and lightning. 'How appropriate!' Josef thought, since the stories meant so much to him, and represented some very important beginnings for him. Marcel even pricked up his ears, since he never heard either of the two stories, and Amelia only knew of vague slivers:

REBECCA AND JOSEF

JOSEF: Girls and women demand attention. They want you to look at them, and then they want to look away. They want to run and they want you to follow. After so many years, it is still the era of boys hunting girls and girls playing at being against boys. I understand this. It is a choice as to what you wish to dedicate your life to: following, or waiting to follow. It is an impulse you can learn to control.

When I went off to college - which Frank Zappa noted was the place to go to get laid, so if you actually want an education you should go to a library - my earliest notions of leading a self-centered existence changed completely. I didn't want to be by myself forever, and the concept of chasing - the pursuit - took me completely. It's all mind games, and if you love tinkering with people's heads for your own delight, I strongly recommend it. My change in perception came due to the close proximity and freedom from oversight - it is the first time everyone is freed from supervision or the need to sneak and hide - so this 'being freed' created a metaphorical frenzy. It isn't the hedonistic wonderland portrayed in the movies, but that image is very popular because that's how people *want* to see it. They ignore the studying, typing, cramming and deadlines as the difficulties they are. It is the sheer closeness of everyone - like Arcosanti - and the convenience - converged with positive fear - of leaving youth, of growing up, of the final scream of debt-free life, of the last hurrah. Some people, as it's been said, never escape high school. Others, it's been said, never really get away from college. Pathetic, truly, but it's a pathetic-ness some of us share.

During my Sophomore Year, I took a class in acting. (*Laughs*.) Yeah. My love of movies made me curious what the other side was like, so between that and (a.) needing the elective credits and (b.) the fact that it fit into my packed schedule, I assumed it would be a breeze. It wasn't, actually: it was horrifying. We were constantly being asked to do things that were ridiculous and humiliating - the Instructor had me sing a song in my "best Italian accent" which was greeted with rolled eyes and snickering and the physical aspects of it were hard to get used to.

She partnered me up with this redhead named Rebecca. I was glad she, personally, divided up the class, but felt added pressure being put with this girl I didn't know and wasn't all that comfortable around.   Rebecca was bright and cheerful and coordinated - her clothing was impeccable, the colors going together stylishly and the tones blending in. She had serious style. So many girls dress poorly and plop on sweatshirts and tight-cut things to make their tits squeeze from the top of their shirt like clay in a Play Doh Factory. Some wear hip huggers that hug a fuckton of hip, have tattoos, obscene piercings - anything in the name of "individuality," but I consider an act of desecration. So this Rebecca is wearing a crisp white shirt with slacks and sandal-shoes or red sweaters with black jeans and boots - every class, something inventive. Honestly … she was just stunning. I know I read a study where appearance matters to women in selecting men - for example, a man wearing a cooking apron is less appealing to them than a man wearing a suit, but a woman wearing a cooking apron or a suit is negligible in a man's view of woman - Rebecca was dressed to kill.

At first, we got along all right - if I saw her walking around I waved or nodded but kept walking, and she would wave back. In class, we didn't say much, but she would laugh sweetly when I stumbled over something or looked like an asshole. I always laughed, too, because I wasn't sure how to react. This one Thursday, we're doing these moronic Situation Drills in which we're supposed to show "genuine affection" for the person we're with in various stages. To make it worse, all were done in front of the class, one at a time. Stage One was a handshake step: we were to walk across the room towards each other - she from the one end, I from the other - make eye contact the entire way, meet in the middle, pause, extend hands, shake hands, walk to the side of the room the other person started at and finally, turn to face the center of the room again. That's all. The Stage Two Event was similar, but along with the handshake we were to verbally greet one another - we would take turns saying Hello, ask a question or issue a formality ("It is a nice day today," "How are you doing?," "Good to see you again") to which the other person would respond succinctly. This was done twice, the first time I had to initiate the conversation, the second time my partner did.

Stage Three was more of the same - crossing from one end to the other, meeting in the middle, but now it involved closer physical contact. In this stage we had to "mutually embrace," hold the embrace, and issue the formality. This, too, happened twice, so each participant was able to start the fleeting conversation. It wasn't meant to be rushed - in fact, if the Instructor felt you were in a big hurry to be done with it you had to do it over and over. While the two of us were locked up in the embrace in the center of the room, subjected to the gaze of the other students I never really knew and the Instructor, I was delighted by her softness - not just of the sweater she had on, but her flesh and her bones, her organs. She was this perfumed, breathing, beating person who was with me, in my arms, and I wasn't sure which of us was hugging the other. But right after we spoke, she let go first, and we walked away from each other. The second time we had to do it, I made positive in my mind that I would release my grip first. In fact, as soon as I said my last, "Fine. Thank you," I immediately dropped my arms and started pacing away. Despite my early release, the Instructor did not make us repeat.

Our Instructor did, however, get even with me with what was to follow - and to this day, I think it was an attempt to embarrass me. I could be wrong. The Impromptu Stage Four was as follows: our Instructor put a chair in the middle of the room where Rebecca was told to sit down. She told me that - and this was my task - I was to, without speaking, *demonstrate* how much I "loved" the girl in the chair. She asked Rebecca if it were okay with her to do the exercise. I'll never forget this: "Work away," she responded. Exact words. So now I'm standing there, and I have to *show* the entire class I care for this girl, that I need her, and I had no idea where to begin. I kneeled next to her and started rubbing her right shoulder - petting, rubbing - and I was met with laughing and giggles. Panicking, I stood up, went around to the back of the chair and started massaging both of her shoulders. "Is this better?" I asked and laughed. No one else thought what I said was funny. Our Instructor, irritated, asked if I'd ever been in love before - "act like that," she emphasized. I told her I've never been in love. She looked stunned. I explained that I was only 19, but to her by 19 your romantic life was over - the love poems were written, the children were generated and the activity in the bed was slowing down. Then she told us class was over - it actually ran a little late - and she just ended Stage Four. Rebecca got up, grabbed her bags and left, along with the rest of the class. My Father always told me that the cruelest things are told in silence, and the silence of the class walking away from me was terribly uncomfortable.

So that class ended and we went on Semester Break for the Holidays and I never thought I'd see Rebecca again. Early in the Spring Semester, however, I caught her in the Student Center and she came over to me and was completely and totally friendly and open and she said to me it was good to see me, and I said it was good to see her, and it's like night-and-day, and I was really caught off-guard, but I went along with it and tried to stay positive. She asked if I was going to the Friday Night Bash being put on by some group and could I go with her. I told her that I had only one class on Fridays - it was in the morning - and the rest of the day I kept completely free. She suggested we meet for lunch since she had nothing to do either and we'd talk. I agreed, and she named the place.

Lunch, though I didn't realize it until now, was part one of what would turn out to be a daylong courtship. We ate light - salads, fruit juice - at this small sit-down diner on campus, and I have to say: the conversation clicked. I opened up about how the Acting Class was a personal catastrophe for me, that I thought our Instructor was some kind of bug-eyed voyeur - she laughed and agreed with me that she was "weirded out" by her - and she seemed to be in total agreement. I asked why she was so cold towards me. I probably shouldn't have said it like that, but I did. Naturally, she became defensive and started explaining how she was having difficulty showing up for classes, maximizing her free time, how hectic her Sorority house was, not to mention some problems at home that were weighing on her. I understood, and told her so, and told her that I thought she was mad at me for not doing the right thing in class, and was worried I made her look bad, which upset me. I wasn't trying to be patronizing, I was trying for honesty. She said I "handled myself well," which I took as a compliment.

After lunch we went to the Lule-Williams Arts Center where they were showing student replicas of Piet Mondrian's works. She wanted to go there and though I didn't know much about art I was just glad lunch was over. We met up with one of her friends, Marushka, there - Marushka had to go to the exhibit for her Art Appreciation class and take a few notes on what she saw. While I thought her being there would be awkward, Marushka and Rebecca tried to include me in on their 'insider conversation,' explaining to me things about people I didn't know but some juicy tidbits they'd done that were incendiary and worth whispering about. All three of us went out to dinner after we watched some television in Marushka's dorm; I volunteered to pay the entire bill but neither would allow it.

Marushka left after dinner to meet up with some other people, leaving just the two of us strolling around the swerving pavements. We debated on what to do to kill time before the party, and we ended up - almost by subconscious will on my part - back in her room with the door shut and me, pacing, looking like I needed to open a window and breathe tree air and regulate myself. We were conveniently the only two people in this part of her Sorority, in the television room, watching the Campus Channel, which was made by the Communications & New Media students and pretty shaky in execution. The two of us sat on the couch, laughing at the technical ineptitude and flubbed lines. I could feel her so close, and breathing, and out of the corner of my eye was watching what she was doing, what she was laughing at. She playfully kicked the side of my leg with her foot, which made me smile. Then she did it again. So I lightly kicked her back. Then she kicked me. Then I kicked a little harder. She told me to take off my sneakers. I asked why. She told me I *had* to. I told her she had to take hers off. She refused. She grabbed me by the collar of my shirt and kissed me on the lips. I basically opened my mouth a little and moved my lips open and shut slowly - they were giving a little effort, but she was the one taking over, her upper lip in my mouth, her lower lip under my lower lip, her tongue grazing the tip of my tongue - the kissing, accompanied by her warm, sweet breath billowing over my flushed cheeks, produced a streaming sensation of tenderness and bliss. I delicately used my fingertips to touch the underside of her jaw, delicately sliding my hands towards her chin and back again, letting my fingers brush her neck. She started to stand up, and so I did, just following along, and before I knew it, I was in her room.

Now, remember I told you last time about her sense of style? That day, for the first time, I saw her wearing a pullover navy blue sweatshirt with a hood that had "Duquesne" on it, and a pair of sweatpants. It was the most dressed-down she could have gotten for me. Not only that, but she wasn't wearing make-up, either - it was very contrary to her image up to that point. I still have no idea why she had a sweatshirt from that particular college on - maybe it was one of the other places she applied to but eventually declined.

She did the undressing for both of us, as we both stood next to her bed. She unbuttoned my clothes, undid my belt, fussed with my pants, my socks, my underpants - after I was disrobed, she pulled off her own sweatshirt and slid down her pants. The entire time she spent stripping the two of us, she never broke eye contact with me, even when she bent down to pull the sweatpants and panties off her feet. The rest was pure automation: touching, fingering, soft kisses. Her face registered enjoyment, and the fact that she looked pleased made me feel like I was doing something right. I was nervous, but it almost didn't matter.

My newness didn't matter to her, and it was never mentioned or inferred - I don't think it was of relevance. She initiated all actions and motions, and this delighted me - I didn't mind her going through the motions, letting me take the passive role. When she held me, or ran her hands along my sides, she was always staring right into me. She kept smiling to keep me smiling, and her movement kept me moving.

When it was over, the two of us just laid there. I wasn't sure what to say or if she felt okay about it or what she wanted to hear from me at that moment, so I waited for her to initiate the conversation. She took her left leg and kicked me. "Now what?" she asked me. I turned to her. You know what I said? "Thank you." She replied, "You're so very welcome." In a little while, she got up out of bed, put on a long t-shirt and the pair of sweatpants on the floor and walked out of the room. She told me she was going to shower and that I should go after her. But I remained still.

The party we wandered into later was like the Epilogue to the Day-Long Courtship, where we went out and talked and laughed, but it was admittedly difficult. Not with anyone else - I had no difficulty talking to other people - but between us, not much was actually said. We danced a little bit, although I admitted to be mediocre at dancing, we drank a lot of beer, but I was so flushed with internal heat and preoccupied with what happened that I still wanted to be in the bed with her, letting the sheets tickle my legs, and not walking around talking and laughing. I felt like I was sharing her with the crowd, with her friends, with some strangers loosely connected to people she knew. I kept trying to read her face to see what she was thinking, but she didn't react to me.

After 1 AM, the night ended with a brief kiss on the lips, and a courteous good-bye. I didn't like the way she reacted to me at the party - I don't know what I expected but what I got didn't please me - and neglected to call her the next day or any day thereafter. That Day, of course, was never repeated. We would see each other, give a brief wave of the arm, but I never had a real conversation with her again. I did see her again at Graduation with her boyfriend, I'm guessing, and she was kind enough to break away from him to come up and give me a strong hug goodbye. I hugged her back. She was the first one to let go, and she was the first one to turn and walk away.

JENNIFER AND JOSEF

JOSEF: Since I was eligible for work-study, I was able to get a job on-campus in Residential Services, where I, along with the other work-study students, made photocopies, phone calls, filled out complaint forms from students who had some kind of problem with their dorm, complaints from students who wanted to change rooms because their roommate(s) were causing problems, complaints from students about the unsanitary nature of the showers. One of the girls I worked with was Jennifer. She was a Business and Finance major from Delaware who came across to me as being calm and even-tempered during the most rushed and stressful of days (which there weren't many of, I can assure you). She and I - since our mini-desks were right by each other, and since we had little to do because the heads of Residential Services were rarely there - had a lot of time to talk and get to know one another. I talked about my family and friends and future plans and campus rumors and the news in general and she did the same - I, despite being notoriously late for everything, was always on time for work the days I knew she was scheduled to be there since I wanted to hear *her* stories and misadventures, like DUI issues and her friends that went overseas to study in Romania or Italy, whichever. The days she wasn't able to show up or she had someone else fill in for her the time slogged by and I took to bringing in newspapers, sandwiches, textbooks and clicking around the Internet just to keep myself occupied. I'd always noticed that most people in college - at that age - are never interested in talking, being friendly or laughing at anything unless they're drunk. A large percentage of people I knew were humorless and bitter corruptibles who had little or no personality unless they were completely intoxicated, which was when the charm finally kicked in. Terrence said our University produced "sophisticated drunks," which is correct, and I'm so glad I never have to see most of them anymore. But I digress.

One night I was with Terrence at this gathering being held off-campus in someone he knew's apartment - it was a four- or maybe even five-bedroom single-floor fortress of sorts, and people were camping inside, mingling on the spacious outdoor patio and hollering obscenities at the ants below, and even carousing the hallways to lean against walls and smoke. It was loud, packed, and clearly a fire hazard. Jennifer happened to be there, and she spotted me first and introduced me to her friend, this squat blonde girl who I still don't know the name of, but seemed cheery. I got the impression from the way she said "I had to meet her" that Jennifer was trying to fix me up with this other girl, because I recall her mentioning her a lot at work, showing me pictures and the like. I don't care for the idea of being set-up; I don't like the idea of strangers communicating through telephone or digital lines about me.

I managed to lose the two of them in the crowd, and I went to the kitchen to mix myself something and proceeded into the living room, which had several couches set up and a Baltimore Orioles/Boston Red Sox game on the television. Bored, I decided to sit there and drink and drink - in between innings, I would get up and go to the kitchen to refill my plastic red cup. I was smart in not mixing beer and liquor like an amateur, but I did drink so much liquor that by the 8th inning I was noticeably wobbling. Sitting still and staring at the television was fine, but moving around was not. Terrence wandered by at some point to tell me he was leaving with this busty blonde girl, and I chuckled and told him to have a good time, and that I'd be leaving soon enough. But I didn't. People came and went, some sat next to me on the couch nursing their drinks because they were just tired of standing, some watched the television with me, but I was a fixture.

Somewhat disgruntled, Jennifer wandered over during the Post-Game discussion to sit next to me on the arm of the sofa and told me that I was leaving with her. "I can't move," I explained, but she grabbed me by the hair and forcefully pulled me out of my seat. She was laughing and stumbling, and when I saw she was going to fall over, I grabbed her by the arm and hoisted her upwards. I looked around for her blonde cohort but she wasn't there - people were asleep on the floor, one right next to the other, and the hallway looked like a convenience store exploded inside of it - seven pools of alcohol filled with raw hot dogs and potato chips were lined up right next to each other, a jar of mustard was smashed along the side walls and smeared everywhere like early primal paintings. We both tip-toed around the pools of beer and shattered glass, so as not to dig our heels into someone's flesh, hair or the broken debris. I asked her where she lived. She pointed down. I told her I needed more information. She gave me basic directions, and using the elevator - filled with half-naked coeds slumped in the corner - we went down and outside into the night.

Her building was only about two blocks away, which was good, but I had trouble standing myself and almost took her with me when I stumbled over a large chain some dipshit stretched across the pavement. She had the key to her building and opened the door and told me to come in, so I did. The place was dark and I asked her where everyone was. "I told you," she said, "*a-broad*. Get me upstairs." I guided her - and myself - up the steps and into her bedroom. I turned on the light switch and we both let out a groan, so I immediately turned it off. I led her to the bed, but as soon as we got there she wrapped her arm around my torso and dragged me down with her and rolled on top of me. Her hand pressed against my face as she leaned over to turn on the small desk light by the bed. "You look just like my Brother," she said, "did I tell you that before?" "I believe so," I told her, and that was when she put her hands around my wrists and was squeezing them. "What? What?" she kept saying while smiling. She started kissing me, and so I started kissing back, but the more I kissed, the harder she kissed.

I had a feeling there was a problem when we started rolling around and I suddenly felt horribly nauseous, while we were gyrating and clawing at each other - and the more she rolled around the more out-of-it I felt, so I relaxed my arms and gave a half-hearted, almost immobile effort. We got our clothes off and she guided me inside of her. I don't know why, but it felt remarkably good - better than ever before. I think the sensation of being physically sick and receiving pleasure simultaneously was what made the feeling so extraordinary. I wanted it to go on forever and at the same time be over immediately.

The next thing I knew, it was eight-something the next morning, the sun was out and I was downstairs, on the couch, wearing nothing but an orange terrycloth bathrobe. I passed out, I guess, with my contact lenses in, so they were stuck to the upper lids of my eyes, and I was having major difficulty seeing. Jennifer was sitting on the floor right in front of where I was laying, completely naked, watching sports highlights on television. She turned to see me on the couch, didn't say anything, got up and went into the kitchen. I asked her how I got downstairs, but she didn't respond. I wandered into the kitchen to find her fixing a bowl of Corn Flakes and taking a can of Milwaukee's Best out of the refrigerator. She opened the can, poured it in the cereal, and started eating with a plastic spoon. I got a bowl from one of the cupboards, and my own spoon, and took some skim milk out of the refrigerator. I sat, poured the cereal into the bowl and added the milk. I started eating, and while eating, inquired as to how she felt. She gave no answer. I asked her how I got downstairs. She gave no answer. When I finished with my cereal I stood up and she, without looking up, said to me, *"Now get the fuck out of this house."* I didn't respond and slowly put the dish in the sink. "I said *fucking NOW*," she screamed, and slammed her open hand on the table. I half-yelled back that I wasn't going anywhere without my clothes, and had to go upstairs to get them, and she yelled, even louder, "*NOW*," pointing to the front door and staring at me with rage. I hastily walked over to the door, where I saw, on a small table by the door, my clothes folded and tied up with string into a neat parcel with a note on top: "JOSEF." I didn't want to stay inside, so I grabbed it, got outside, took the parcel around the corner behind a tree, cut my hand open scrambling to break off the string, put my pants on and my shirt, tossed the bathrobe on the ground and walked home … in my bare feet. She didn't leave my shoes and I didn't go back to get them.

I also quit my easy job with Residential Services to avoid her. I still don't know why she was so mad at me. Did I do something wrong? I asked Terrence what he thought and he said I should have left immediately instead of lingering around, tipsy or not. He thought I took advantage of her, which …

come to think of it, I probably did. I didn't look at it like that, but I probably knew that taking her home would lead to that.

I never did see her again, though, and didn't dare ask anyone what they knew of her.

16.

The Troupe, as they drove over the scenic bridge that rose above Lake Pontchartrain, were pleased, for once, to see something other than tree lines, blue road markers and diffident billboards. Arkansas looked like Virginia and Virginia looked like Pennsylvania - it was when they crossed the long bridge rising over the lake that they realized how sterile those previous images had been. Above the calm water there were dark, purplish washes of watercolor streaked across the sky. Marcel was grateful the sun had been negated for once, since his eyes were sore from squinting through some of the accumulated glare of the past several days and the refracted light bouncing off the speeding items surrounding them.

As promised, Josef made the phone call to Terrence about getting around the city and where to keep the tractor-trailer for safety. Terrence, on the other end of the line, agreed to ask around and told Josef to call back when they were closer to town so he could give them parking and walking directions. Within a half hour, Terrence did follow through on his promise and told Josef he called someone he met from town who called someone else, and by making the personal connection he could park the truck in the corner of a Private Lot for $20 a day. Terrence offered to pay the entirety of the fee, which Josef told him he needn't do but thanked him nonetheless for the small gesture. He kept Terrence on the phone for navigation directions through the city and where, precisely, the Private Lot was located and said he'd call for a taxi for them to take them to the apartment.

The Custom Travel Booklet became temporarily superfluous as Josef relayed the necessary information to Marcel the driver, so Amelia set the Booklet aside temporarily giving up her role as navigator and instead sat nervously as Marcel swerved around to avoid potholes, people and medians. The Private Lot was three or four miles from Terrence and Josef's apartment, and getting into the lot was not a problem - there was a young man standing there in a cockeyed red baseball hat who knew they were coming and told them where they could safely park. After getting out and stretching, Cameron checked his watch and marveled at the time they were making - it was only 2 PM. Josef and Marcel grabbed all of Josef's frozen bags from the trailer and closed up the tractor-trailer for it to rest and collect itself. The taxi arrived in fifteen minutes.

Terrence was waiting outside the door of the apartment, waiting for them. When the taxi stopped, he paid the driver (everyone said he didn't have to), gave a $5 tip, and picked up some luggage. Josef quickly introduced everyone to Terrence, and vice versa, though no one could shake hands because all hands were on bags. Simple nods and basic eye contact were sufficient.

The apartment, while clean, was almost eerily barren - Terrence, like Josef, detested hauling excessive furniture, and the few things that were brought did not fill up much of the space they were allotted. Amelia, not much of an interior decorator, offered advice on putting prints or framed posters on some walls to add 'life,' maybe some extra chairs, a coffee table book on a coffee table. Terrence talked about mooching some tables from someone he met that had no need for them, but would wait and see. Josef's few boxes of books, albums, tapes and ephemera were stacked neatly in one corner waiting for him to unravel and sort. The sight of them crumpled up made him nervous.

The only decorative indulgence Terrence had time to work on was the tacking up of strings of Christmas lights along the walls and ceilings, hanging-dipping-rising in certain spots, with strands of white covering the outline of the doorways and bathroom and swirling around the kitchen. The idea came to him when he sat in a bar and saw that the only source light they had was from dozens upon dozens of strings in a similar arrangement haphazardly thrown everywhere - the lights provided enough glow so that you could keep off the high-powered ceiling lights and other ocular disturbances while enjoying cold beverages.

TERRENCE: The waitress at this place told me it's just great mood lighting, and that she had them in her apartment, too. So I thought ... (*Shrugs*)

Since it was 3:30 and no one had lunch, Terrence took them to Pat O'Brien's on Bourbon Street to eat an early meal and then get dessert later on. Instead of taking a taxi they opted to walk. While they walked, Josef talked with Terrence about this and that - Terrence was the Informationalist, getting him the inside track on some of the things he found out while Marcel, Amelia and Cameron played Tourist, gazing upwards at the architecture, the oil lamps and the contrast between the French Quarter and the looming Business District, which towered above them. The sky constantly threatened to rain any minute and Cameron was groaning about not having a hat on while Amelia groaned about not having her Pentax K-1000 with her.

At Pat O'Brien's they were told there would be a ten-minute wait, so they stood in the dank hallway and chatted to pass the time. Josef brought Terrence up-to-date on the stories they'd been telling up to that current fraction of time, the rules and regulations of said storytelling and that he was the last contributor. Terrence said he had a story to contribute, but would save it for dinner.

The five of them were seated next to a rather austere fountain flowing green with absinthe - there was a tall waitress standing nearby with a small booth offering almost thimble-sized glasses of the drink for a nominal fee. Everyone at the table ordered the crawfish étouffée based on the waitress' recommendation and all - sans Marcel - opted to start the night off early (it was 5 o'clock somewhere) with mint juleps ("Like in *The Great Gatsby*," remarked Cameron).

Terrence spoke about his minimal time in Louisiana, some of the oddballs and class acts he'd met and a few places he wanted to head to in the next few weeks before the next semester officially started. Amelia told him about their plans on the West Coast. When all became quiet, Terrence felt like it was the time for his anecdote:

THE HI-POTION

TERRENCE: My Father always got these magazines from the Marines in the mail - this was the *Marine Corps Times*, I believe - and I was flipping through the newest issue while over at their house for Thanksgiving. In the back of the magazine was this ad from this Company, *The Self-Improvement Network for Men* that was selling this, well, what they called a "Magic Love Potion" that offers a 100% Guarantee that it will work. What it said was, and there are these marketing inserts of stern-looking men and women in lab-coats and names with titles, like "Dr. Christopher Lalancette, M.D." and "Professor Kristen Blum, Ph.D." who were from obscure research facilities I've never heard of. It had testimonials in a size 8 font from generic-sounding people and a lot of instructions: you send them $49.99, they send you a bottle of these "pheromones" that you pour into your cologne with a funnel - which came with it - spray it on, go out and *presto* more attention, guaranteed women around you. I asked my Dad for the article and he told me to take the entire magazine. I wanted to show it to a bunch of people.

Now, I took more than my share of Psychology courses - I double majored in it and Chemical Engineering - and this thing sounded like a giant hoax. I showed it to my friends back home and they all wanted to get it. We laughed about it, and thought of it as a joke, you know, like Sea Monkeys, Pet Rocks and all the Great Fads, and we were curious to try some, on a lark, and see how it worked. So, all three of us - my friend Peter, his Brother Simon and I each wrote checks and waited for our packages to arrive.

If we were going to do this truly scientifically, there would have to be a control group, accurate data, variables and a slew of other relevant and plausible pieces - so trying this was just in good, amateur fun. One constant among all three of us was that we were single at the time - I had broken up with my girlfriend a few months earlier and so had Pete. Simon was looking and following but nothing official.

Our shipments came two weeks later, in tiny cardboard boxes, and all of us planned to try it together on the same exact night after we all took showers and used the same type of soap (Dial) and shampoo (Dove). I took my bottle of Calvin Klein cologne, poured in a measured amount and sprayed myself three times: back of knee, wrists, neck. I gave the same bottle to Peter and he sprayed himself in the same three places, as did Simon. So there was one well-planned detail: all three of us used the same Magic Love Potion - mine, for starters - the same fragrance and all of us sprayed the same amount.

That night, we also tried to dress similar - long sleeve shirts, dress pants, appropriately colored shoes. Wearing identical clothes would have been embarrassing. Also, appearance-wise and personality-wise, there was nothing we could do: Peter can be pleasant at times and insufferable at others, Simon has a habit of going for snide come-backs instead of more considerate and playful retorts ... and Christ knows what flaws I have. These factors could not be fixed. Facially, that's another God-granted gift: some women may delight in bushy eyebrows, while most would probably be repulsed. It depends.

Skipping over the middle act - because the middle is always the most dispensable part of relationships and conversation; the impulse of act one bleeds into act three and the let-down - I can only tell all of you this: somehow, something somewhere worked. All three of us - yes, all of us - left the last club in the wee small hours with three delightful and euphoric ladies we'd met and spent the entire night talking to them. Simon was floored by his luck, and a few days later when all of us met up for lunch, he was almost speechless. We dissected the incident piece by miniscule piece. Before claiming this was a miracle drug - or scent - I suggested we test it out again and again. Simon shrugged and just rationalized that it worked, while Peter and I put our heads together to make sense of it. Yes, it could have been pure chance - we could have been more charming than usual and we could have been dressed better than usual. One thing we never considered was the fact that the last club was one we'd never been to before. Maybe it was always teeming with women. Maybe we were more confident and forward than usual because we knew, in the back of our minds, that this scent of mating was emanating from us. (*Laughs*) It could have been just about anything. Luck, even.

So we tested it out some more. Such and such night we wore the cologne, and were successful. Another night we decided not to use it at all. Simon put up the biggest fuss when Peter and I decided to not use it - he said, "Why are we going out without putting it on if it can be a little helpful? We could just waste the night." In the long run, it didn't always work for all of us - I had contemplated tinkering with the cologne, replacing the treated cologne with a freshly-bought untreated bottle and never letting on - but, I have to admit, it *seemed* that the nights we wore it, we were more 'successful' - by our own standards - than the nights we did not use it. I don't have precise numbers, even though I tried to draw some up, and I don't know enough about all the details to come to a conclusion that works in my head.

But I have to say, I don't want to believe that a bottle of real or unreal chemicals made in a lab, when applied to my skin and sensed by another person, is what makes the difference between her and I becoming personal and her and I remaining strangers. I wouldn't want to think that this is all it takes, that it's all so primal and has so little to do with choice as much as biology. It troubled and intrigued me so much I would have loved to really study it further, to really debunk it. It also troubled me that I would want to, in the first place, use such a talisman, since my decision to try it - and that of my friends - speaks volumes about us. I was left with more questions than answers, hoax or no hoax.

After dinner, they put the remnants of their drinks in plastic cups - it's the law around town, apparently - and paraded around the French Quarter, led by Terrence with his flute, pointing out some spots they could check out later on. As it got later, the streets filled with more and more ruffians, tourists, scoundrels over 40, families, drunks, college students and the elderly into a mosh pit of fumbling bedlam - the music blaring from the clothing shops clashed with the music from the clubs which clashed with the sound of people yelling and dancing - it was festive and smothering, and it was only 8 PM. The Troupe took in the sights and smells and anarchy as they made the crawl from one establishment to another, pulling out Driver's Licenses every new place, getting different, high-powered, vase-shaped glasses with green or blue liquor inside of them - none of that carbohydrate-heavy *beer* nonsense - watching and mingling, separating for a time and then reforming into a small huddle once more.

Around 10 PM, at yet another bar whose landscape was really no different than the other places they were at and contained virtually the same volume of people, Marcel and Josef sat at the bar next to a burly, bearded man smoking a locally-rolled full-sized cigar on one-side and three cops in full uniform at the table right next to the bar, each with a can of cola in front of them that they continuously refilled with some beverage out of a Thermos under the table. Terrence left to go talk to a group of barflies he knew while

Marcel and Josef watched Cameron and Amelia skitter and shake around the dance floor, bathed in light and haze, jerking their elbows outward and looking exactly like every other dancing couple in the room. Josef, having consumed too many Pineapple Explosions - a drink that contained both pineapple juice and a lot of rum - had already switched to decaf coffee, and Marcel was still nursing the only drink he ordered all evening, a Manhattan on the rocks. Both of them were tired beyond comprehension, but confessed to each other that they were happy to be anywhere but home. "I have to stay," Josef added, "but what else would I do to kill time? *One must never stagnate!*"

After a brief discussion on the long walk back to Terrence's apartment, Marcel, Amelia and Cameron agreed to spend the next day in town for a Pacing Break of their own and to see some of the sights: it's been said that a location's secrets are discovered by those passing by quickly. Terrence said he'd be glad to keep them as long as needed, and tried to encourage them to spend the remainder of the week. The three said they'd take it one day at a time, ruling by committee.

Space was at a minimum in the apartment, and 1 AM was not the best time to try to organize anything. Josef took charge by granting Amelia her own room - the spare room, his room - and Terrence could keep his own bedroom. Using a handful of thumbtacks, eight clothespins, a ball of twine and four crisp white bed sheets he divided the room into Quadrants I, II, III and IV, with Quadrant IV being the Television Quadrant, which no one would sleep in. Quadrant I was granted to Josef, II to Cameron and III to Marcel, and within the individual Quadrants each person was granted a minimal amount of quiet and privacy.

All were trying to sleep but most just laid in their respective Quadrants in their underwear and soiled t-shirts and looked at the ceiling or stared at the flickering lights swirling around the walls, blinking, twinkling, shining. The shining/flashing reminded Josef of the Tony Conrad film *The Flicker*, so he tried concentrating on the on-off sequence in hopes of being transported to unconsciousness. Marcel didn't even bother, and wandered into the kitchen area quietly, tiptoeing and cautious as to not step on feet or legs. Already in the kitchen, eating a bowl of shredded wheat, was Terrence, who felt hungry, and Cameron, who was playing with his half-glass of apple juice and leaning against the refrigerator.

TERRENCE: It makes me feel good none of you can sleep either.

CAMERON: I felt tired an hour ago but now I could run a marathon. Alcohol has this strange stimulant effect on me. It makes everyone else sleepy but me. I can't stop my pulse from racing.

MARCEL: Over the counter sleeping medications keep me awake. Those Alka-Seltzer Night Time Tablets for colds give me the same feeling, like something horrible is going to happen.

CAMERON: (*To Terrence*) You swear you have no Red Rose tea? Mint?

TERRENCE: No coffee. Hate the taste.

CAMERON: What do you do in the morning to wake up, then?

TERRENCE: I'm never tired in the morning.

CAMERON: Luck-y.

Marcel sat down on one of the kitchen stools.

MARCEL: I have to tell you, this is a great apartment in a great location.

TERRENCE: (*Pause*) I'm slowly getting used to it.

MARCEL: You're going to get your ... Master's Degree, right?

TERRENCE: (*Nodding*) That and hopefully more. It's going to cost me. But ... it's better than working.

Everyone in the kitchen agreed. When everyone stopped talking, all of them looked around at objects in the room half-illuminated, half in shadow.

MARCEL: You know, I meant to ask you earlier but didn't get the chance to talk to you about your girlfriend, because I swore you said you had one at dinner. How did she feel about you coming down here without her?

TERRENCE: I broke up with her two weeks before I left. I turned in my notice. She wanted to keep the whole long-distance thing going but I thought it would be an anchor for both of us. And honestly, helping her cope with her innumerable problems was just weighing me down. We would meet for breakfast or, hell, any meal, and she would either complain about her coworkers or her friends or her family and her Sister. Mostly her Sister. Everything was always wrong, and she'd call me at 2 in the morning just *hysterical* and tell me that her Sister's boyfriend was beating her up, and that her Sister just called her. I don't know why she had to tell me. Did she think *I* was going to do something about it? Then she'd, at the end of the call, moan about me about the job I had. I was working landscaping, and this just shamed her to no end. I got fired from my other job for being late half a dozen times, and a friend of mine ran the business and helped me out. She told me she was going to squeeze me into the mailroom at the rest home - she's a nurse, by the way. I lied and told her that the job was good for the time being. But then she was like, "You're a goddamn engineer. Engineer yourself a job that isn't *grass cutting*." (*Takes breath*) It was good to be with her ... at first, but ... it became a problem. It wasn't genuine. She usually didn't want to. I had to talk her out of her pants like we were in fucking junior high. It was, "My friends hate me, I want to get married, we should get married" or "I'm turning 28, my Mom's asking me if I'd be married by 30, does that sound reasonable to you?" She fought me on it. Then she said, "Okay, let's get engaged before you leave." She wanted to go to the Bahamas or something like that. I couldn't. (*Pause*) I can't.

MARCEL: Was she always like that?

TERRENCE: No, at first she would ask about me, and I'd ask about her. But she, I guess, got used to me and before I knew it she was criticizing me. Get this: she said I looked "scroungy" and "unkempt" and kept buying me new clothes. Now, I have to confess, I did enjoy tormenting her. I would package up the clothes that she bought without my consent and mail them back to her house. I would say I was going to show up and pick her up at 5 PM and actually get there at 6 or even 7:30, just to start an argument. We were not compatible. I can admit that now.

17.

Deciding subconsciously to sleep in, the Troupe + 1 arose, showered, ate some oatmeal and threw on clean clothes from their personal bags. Terrence wanted to go over to Tulane with Josef to show him around - Josef was nervous and eager to investigate where things were, leaving Cameron, Amelia and Marcel to stroll around town. They all named places that they wanted to see, shops they wanted to look in that Terrence had no interest in and some wanted to enjoy the day of sober sight-seeing. Terrence gave them a small folding map of the streets and some local attractions.

One of the benefits of daytime wandering the relative quiet - the downtown shops and packed art galleries had rough looking blue dogs painted on the windows displaying no tact or inventiveness and jewelry stores selling vain and expensive bobbles were all explored in stride. The town, in a way, reminded Amelia of New Hope back in Pennsylvania with its art-intensive posturing and upper-class self-pride - ironic, when you think of it, since the tourist part of the city is so gimmick-heavy, cheap and low class: a parody of sex. There are t-shirts with crass sayings on Bourbon St. and handcuffs and talking dildos and other gadgets relating to intercourse, but the intent is not serious and the taboo-ness of the act is purposely demystified. But in the demystification a certain joy is dismissed as well, an integral mystery to the allure of the act and the cosmic importance of the act. Marcel kept noticing all of this, and was somewhat saddened by it - Amelia and Cameron observed but offered little commentary.

With a plan to mark off where they'd been, the trio lazily sought out the attractions while keeping an active eye for minute details. In front of the street-performing blues guitarist with an acoustic guitar, two Asian teenagers danced and skipped to the beat: the guitarist paid them no mind and continued plucking the strings. When they became tired of prancing about, they dropped a few bills in the man's guitar case. He did not react.

Cameron was firmly intent on walking to Harrah's to play some slots and no one objected. They spent a half-hour inside, tossing a few quarters into the machines but getting very little pay-off (no pellets, in other words). The very instant Cameron hit twenty quarters on the one machine he was playing, he scooped up the change with both hands, stuffed the money into his pockets and insisted on leaving. "I want to walk out a winner," he joked.

At lunch, none of the three were particularly hungry but Amelia wanted to try some beignets and have a café au lait with it - the local breakfast/snack/tourist meal - so they wandered by the mall built along the Mighty Mississippi to browse through some of the stores and eat their sugary food. Cameron wandered off from the pack to look in the boot store while Marcel and Amelia took their meal trays outside where tables with umbrellas were lined up.

While seated, they listened intently to a conversation this one woman was having with herself but without looking directly at her. She was seated at a table directly behind them and was wearing a giant brown cowboy hat - in each of the three other seats at her table were enormous garbage bags filled with unknown things. On the table sat a cup of coffee.

WOMAN: ... that's what I said, I said, *it's not good to do that now* or ever. (*Pause*) He cares about you and that's all you did for him? But (*Pause*) do not criticize him too harshly. (*Pause*) Why can't I enjoy the peace that always follows you? Why? I enjoy only the past, that's why.

Never the present. (*Pause*) Well, studying the world taught you everything you know. I have not given up the hope of happiness for you and him. It will work out. (*Pause*) I, listen to me now, it will work out. (*Pause*) Just follow your head, like you've always done. (*Pause*) What? It's not the same for me. No, it's not the same....

When Cameron did come outside with his food and drink, Amelia gestured to him not to stare at the table behind them and not to sit facing the woman that was talking aloud. He did as he was told, and slowly ate while listening to the woman's voice. All of their eyes were glued to the table, the pastries and the pigeons, circling around their feet and waiting for falling crumbs. After they left cleaned up their places and brushed some food onto the pavement, they waved to the woman, who was still talking to the air, and she waved back to them. All three agreed that if they didn't know better, they'd have thought the woman was having an actual conversation on the telephone.

———————————————————

At dinner, when Amelia, Cameron and Marcel reunited with Josef and Terrence in a smaller sausage-sandwich and beer place, the topic of marriage came up:

AMELIA: So I'm taking it that all five of us want to get married or have a life partner someday.

Some nodded, some shook heads.

JOSEF: Marriage has become something of a joke, though.

MARCEL: *Something* of a joke? That's funny.

JOSEF: With all that divorce and marital problems and children being raised by a single parent ... it just doesn't hold bearing anymore. People don't want to be alone, so they get married, but once they're married, they don't like the person they're married to. No one sticks it out anymore because society says they don't have to.

TERRENCE: I went through, as a teenager, my parents' messy divorce, and seeing how brutal that was changed my view on marriage early on.

TERRENCE'S FAMILY

TERRENCE: My parents started arguing back when I was in middle school - it couldn't have been over money since they were both earning a lot. It would be simple things, like where dishes were placed the night before or on what side of the driveway someone's car was temporarily parked. Meaningless stuff. They didn't see each other often, either. They both worked long hours and wouldn't get home until 7 or 8 o'clock - my Grandfather, who lived alone a few blocks away in his own spacious house, would bring over dinner for my Brother and myself - that is, until my Brother went off to Annapolis just to get out of the house and make grace with the sea, and then it was just me. I looked forward to him visiting over the Holidays, but he rarely did come home - he would always call to say he was spending, say, Thanksgiving with a new girlfriend, or New Year's with a group of friends in Manhattan.

Strangely, I was unaffected by the fighting between my parents on a personal level - it bothered me, sure, but it wasn't like I was the referee, either, and their arguments were almost never over me. The two of them may have really loved each other at first, as most people usually do, but something ominous set in, and the sight of each other sickened them.

I think the reason why I was so unfazed was that I was a little older. When I look back at my early childhood - the so-called 'formative years' - I have no regrets and I don't hold either of them to blame. Someone at some point in time told me I should feel some resentment, but I don't. They never hit or abused me, they never went through my belongings and they always made sure I went to good schools. When some minor crisis came up, like when I needed to take Speech classes because one of my teachers realized I couldn't say "snake" properly - my version sounded like "thhhhnake" - my Dad, I remember, was the one who eased my fears and told me to stop crying and that there was nothing wrong with me. My one Uncle needed Speech classes too, he said, and he's fine. It made me feel better when I found out someone I knew had the same problem and resolved it.

But the disillusion of their relationship could have been seen well ahead of time, and it was inevitable things would fall apart. I knew it, they knew it. I don't want want to go into every development because I don't remember them all and it's not worth thinking about. Their relationship simply had a timeline, and I believe all relationships do. After some point, you have to realize it's over instead of prolonging the misery together. By the time they were throwing things at each other and screaming, I'd get up and leave, go to my room and practice guitar. When my Brother was around he'd intervene and yell at both of them, but that just made them raise their voices louder.

I do know that one thing that comforted me was that my then girlfriend Silvana's parents were going through significantly worse. Her Dad was cheating on her Mom with her Mom's Step-Sister, her Mom would drive over to her Sister's apartment building, see her husband's car and slash the tires, that sort-of thing. A lot of people I knew dealt with that. The fact that I had it comparatively easy was a morbid comfort.

When it came time, I went away to school with the money saved up for me from both of them. They did not want me to have debt coming out of school, debt to start my life with, and I was overwhelmingly grateful. I still try to talk to them. I talked to Mom long ago to tell her about my Graduate Studies, and she told me that she was proud. Dad's a little harder to get a hold of, but when I do talk to him he always tells me I have to call my Mother regularly, and that I should check up on my Brother, too. Neither of them got remarried, and Mom lives with her Sister and Dad has a girlfriend that he refuses to talk to me about, saying he doesn't want me to be mad at him for doing it, and that the less I know about his girlfriend the better. He told me he'd never marry her, and that she knows it. "It's an antiquated tradition," he said to me. My parents' relationship always made me second-guess myself: If I get married, will the friendship that's supposed to develop after the love dies blossom, or will it all turn to hate?

While watching Terrence use his Credit Card to pay for a round of shots for the table, Cameron wondered where his money was coming from - he spent a large sum the previous night running up a tab and paid that off with plastic, and there he was again, charging it. Did Terrence get an inheritance from his parents of the kind that allowed for such free spending? Cameron was grateful he did not have to open up his own wallet for spirits, but the splurging on Terrence's part made him uncomfortable. Josef pleaded with him to stop - that everyone could pay for his or her own refreshments - but Terrence waved him off. Not wanting to ruin the mood or begin arguing, he shirked away from potential conflict.

Outside, there were a string of Street Acts being performed that had amassed large cramped crowds - on blankets tossed on the uneven asphalt were several women in loose-fitting sequins dresses and tiny red top hats held on with rubber bands giving blow jobs to men laying prone and quiet. The women were moving slowly but with intent, their eyes never breaking contact with the men alongside of them. The acts ran in a row as far as the eye could see: tourists, voyeurs, locals and couples were walking up and down the unending line observing the different pairings like figures in glass casings at the museum. Marcel looked up above and saw viewers leaning down from the wrought-iron balconies above, armed with handheld movie cameras, binoculars or just seeing with their own eyes. Amelia watched for a little before wandering off to the bar across the street that sold a raspberry-flavored drink in a bright red plastic container shaped like a boot; Josef admired the self-control of the men and the patience of the women.

That night, in their Quadrants, Josef slept soundly while Cameron, Marcel and Amelia mulled around the kitchen picking at candy pieces in a glass bowl and filling up their mugs with orange juice. They decided it would be best to leave, to get on, mainly because of the cacophonous atmosphere and Terrence's charge account. Amelia snuck back and peeked in Terrence's room to see if he was asleep and to keep him up-to-date on their impromptu plans, but figured they'd just drop it on him in the morning. In the meantime, all three snuck into the unused Quadrant IV, in the left-most corner of the divided room, to huddle together with a bag of pretzels and channel surf with the mute on and the Closed Captioning feature activated so the show's transcript was printed on the bottom of the screen.

18.

Despite having spent only a finite amount of time in New Orleans, Marcel, Amelia and Cameron all agreed it was a fine, compelling city, but living there might not be so desirable - some of the outskirts looked rancid and festering, and the sporadic rain was a constant irritant.

Terrence and Josef were visibly disappointed by their hasty departure, but both understood their desire to move on and continue west, young wo/man. Terrence, in particular, tried to get them to stay by saying they should take some of the local tours or visit the swamps, but they politely declined. A taxi was called, everyone shook hands, Amelia hugged all as Amelia had a tendency to do, and they took their carpetbags, studied the basic Exit Directions and prepared to drift away.

The man at the Parking Lot was paid his fee in tens and they became reacquainted with the tractor-trailer.

CAMERON: (*Inquiring*) Are you sure your delivery is okay in there?

MARCEL: Oh, this thing is top-of-the-line. You could keep dead bodies back there.

CAMERON: I'll remember you said that.

On the highway out of New Orleans, driving past and through waterlogged greenery and concrete and metal rising out of tepid waters, they debated how well Josef would tolerate being so far from Pennsylvania and how he would get along with Terrence. None remembered to ask him what he thought of the school once he took the Tour with Terrence and why he didn't visit the campus earlier instead of taking Terrence on his word, accepting admission and plopping in. Marcel did not ask him - again

- why he 'copped out' and not followed his artistic desires, like everyone knew he was capable of doing. The trouble was, they couldn't find time to pull him aside and talk to only him. If he was pleased with being there, he didn't show it, but in typical Josef fashion he could have simply been pessimistic about his own rapture.

Amelia offered to take up a running bet to see how long he would stay before just ditching his school agenda and moseying back home on the glass saddle. Marcel asked for specifics on her running bet. For example: would he visit home for a short while, on break, and then drop out, or would he wait it out and leave after the first year, and, if he did decide to leave, how would he get back East: driving? flying? Marcel could hear Josef, in his heart of hearts, ranting on his own preferred form of transportation:

JOSEF: (*Frustrated*) America does not have an adequate system of speed trains which it so sorely needs. This is a major liability. The current set-up, which is clunky and amalgamated, is a disgrace. America, in many ways, consistently contradicts itself. For example, it obsesses over its own health while overeating and wasting its bodies. It frets over illness but is fearful of its own doctors. America claims it wants to support free speech, but condemns people who speak freely and demand an apology. It wants a clean environment but ruins the environment with fumes and chemicals from its factories. America wants to get everywhere in a hurry, but waits in line to get there - just like the cattle-lines at Disney World and shopping centers. With a proper system of speed trains across the country, you could save time, money and the environment. You could slow down the construction of new highways through forests and nature and people's back yards. The original trains were neglected with the advent of the plane, the automobile and, well, massive tractor-trailers for mass transportation of goods. The train, too, is communal and enclosed whereas the car is autonomous and completely personal. The ads you see for automobiles emphasize that point: rugged individuality in a desolate land, power, speed, men and/or women trailblazing through a path of their own choosing. But, ironically, they are not choosing their own path - their path is actually chosen for them. Face it: like a living saint once said, *it's all one road.*

As the tractor-trailer ventured into the Lone Star State, the three remaining members of the Troupe, enjoying the extra space in the cabin due to the absence of Josef (but, of course, missing Josef), chewed on submarine sandwiches and bright red cola they bought at the convenience store where they also filled up on gas. While the scenery up to Louisiana had been frighteningly similar, in Texas the trees dwindled down to a finite number and the highway sat smack in the middle of enormous, primitive land. Billboards from the East were eliminated, and the traffic had been drastically minimized - the swarms of cars and motor homes and motorcycles and children in backseats watching cartoons on drop-down screens and wives staring intently at maps while their husbands slouched in their seats were few to the point of being nearly extinct. Even fellow truck drivers had apparently stopped a long while ago. The plates of the few vehicles they did come across, which were being examined by Marcel, were no longer from all over the country - in Texas, the plates were mostly from Texas, with a few from Arkansas and Louisiana.

The endless Béla Tarr-esque flatland - deprived of color or flavor - had nothing to prove: its ordinariness evoked boredom in the three and their concentration, even mid-day and after spoonfuls of sugar and caffeine, was suffering because of it. Marcel revealed:

MARCEL AND SADIE REX

MARCEL: I worked at the Grace Kelly Memorial Library for about a year, and as all of you probably remember, I loved the job. I was interviewed to do something completely different than what I ended up working at - they really needed someone to help with computer issues and do some programming, but I was qualified for neither. My Mother knew the Head of the Library, Mrs. Whitmore, who initially interviewed me for the computer job that I was completely unqualified for. I explained to her I only knew a small amount of computer things and wasn't all that interested in learning about them beyond what I already knew. She told me it would be fine, and I'd get the hang of it. I reluctantly agreed, since my delivery job had been rendered obsolete and I had no other real offers. Mrs. Whitmore put me under the care of Bradley, the Head Administrator, a paunchy young dilettante with rosy apple cheeks who appeared civil at first but felt being handed an assistant was too troublesome for him to even begin to contemplate. Mrs. Whitmore felt I would learn best under Bradley's supervision and that the burden was too much for him to shoulder alone. But Bradley took his unhappiness out on me, asking me questions about things I did not have valid answers for - pertaining to the finer workings of a network and the countless acronyms that are tied to it - and then rolling his eyes and letting out an exhaust of air from his barely opened mouth. Once he regained his composure, he spoke very slowly to me, explaining it like a parent physically and verbally restraining him-or-herself from issuing a tongue-lashing to a head-in-the-clouds young liar.

Brad brought in books from his own collection on computers that he requested I take home and study during my 'free time' - these became a nice little stack in my bedroom that I stuffed in one corner and set dirty dishes and cups on that were no longer needed by me. When I came in the next day he would grill me about the finer points. I played stubborn and became nasty. After two weeks, Whitmore asked to speak to me privately. I told her I couldn't stand this Brad character, that he was being difficult with me and that I would rather interact with people and work at the main check out pavilion. The idea of me with many people made her hesitant, and then she changed her tune, as in "I'll talk to Bradley for you" and "Things will work out." I secretly found this to be insulting.

I was moved after some deliberation. At my new post I felt better and less cooped up, and no one bothered me. Before, all the servers and equipment were stacked high in a room that was architecturally designed to be a closet, and here I was back in open spaces and free to interact and sit and relax. I found the opportunity to be around the public liberating and nerve-wracking.

Kaye was the woman who showed me the details of working the computers - how to scan the Library Card Barcode, the book(s) and the assorted media, then run them past a manila-colored box so the items would not set off the alarms when the patron left. I was also shown how to work the cash register if a patron wished to pay off any late fees. All in all, the front desk was a lot simpler than the previous job since I didn't have to crack a manual to figure it out.

When the checkout lines were slow and I had nothing to do, I was allowed to read at my seat. Well, I don't know if *allowed* is appropriate, but I would look around at the other workers and elderly volunteers on check out duty and that's what they would do. Some days were exceptionally slow and afforded me a great chance to go through the poetry shelves and the oversized art bookshelves - I'd get books on Balthus and Egon Schiele and flip through them at my leisure.

Once or twice I would try to say something to a volunteer or one of the staff, but they were curt and did not want to talk. I wanted to know about them, how they got there; I wanted to ask the older man I saw on Thursdays about the service medals pinned on a green cap he never took off, but his (and their responses) were lethargic and short - they either had nothing to say or just didn't want to be bothered. It didn't hurt, because they never talked to each other, either. One mole-like man had a noticeable habit of exhaling strongly through his nose like a cartoon bull any time he had to get off his seat and check some patron's materials. Most of the ladies were either scurrying about moving items from one vacant spot to the other or sitting alone reading *Vanity Fair* - the magazine, not Thackeray.

But being a check out person had many bright points, and that was interacting with or examining an odd assortment of characters and bizarre types that would pass by daily. One particular homeless man used to come in periodically, sit in the 1st Floor Reading Area and snore loudly. Other times he would spend a lengthy amount of time in the bathroom where he would wash his clothes. I went into the bathroom one day and saw him. He said hello to me and I said hello to him. The police no longer came when we called them over, saying that he was harmless and that he should be left alone. In an ironic and surreal moment, he came rushing over to the checkout desk one nameless day and claimed to have found a $20 bill by the magazine section and handed it over to one of the volunteers, who put it in the register. Why didn't he keep it? He could have used it more than anyone else.

One regular library user would come in every Wednesday at 2 PM: Sadie Rex. She was lively, cute and intelligent. She went to Temple but lived in an apartment complex close to the library. She would always come to me to check out because I made it a point to wave her down and tell her to stop by and talk. It started when she got out these four items:

Berger, John. Ways of seeing. London: Penguin Books, 1972.

Brooks, Paul. The house of life: Rachel Carson at work; with selections from her writings published and unpublished. Boston: Houghton, Mifflin, 1972.

Davis, Miles. In a silent way. New York: Columbia, 1969.

Lear, Linda J. Rachel Carson: witness for nature. New York: H. Holt, 1997.

... and upon seeing them on the counter, I remarked how pleasantly odd it was to see those particular items together. She lit up and gave some reason for "trying out" each piece. I started seeing her routinely - pretty much every Wednesday - and got to talking about this new item or that new item - nothing long, only a few minutes. I took an interest in her and began looking forward to the moments in which we exchanged words. Each week, with every new collection of diverse items, I asked her more questions: about her, about why she chose this particular library when there were so many in Philly, about how she liked Temple. I was building - in my mind - her story up to the point I met her using these details. I also used the books she read as a syllabus for myself to follow. I kept note of what she checked out in a tablet, and as soon as she would return them I always got to them first, checked them back into the system and then checked them out again with my Library Card. I saw it as a chance to learn what she was learning and educate myself in the process.

So one Wednesday she came in, and she's not alone - she's with this heavy-set guy with a crew cut and a goatee and the two of them wander around looking for books and things together. I followed both of them with my eyes. I stared them down. They walked over to me with a handful of things. She's warm and pleasant as usual. He's standing with her, but doesn't say anything. I kept looking at him. "Oh," she said to me, "this is *my* Rob." *My*. Possession. I nodded. She went on about something-or-other. I didn't say anything. I looked at the computer screen. After I ran her items through the system, I stacked them in a pile and pushed them towards her. I made it clear this made me upset. She knew something was up. So the following week, she returned, alone, and walked up to my counter. Again, I was very cold to her. I wouldn't talk much. Showing up to work, then, became an ordeal. Meeting decent women in this day and age is difficult. So many are damaged, neurotic and demanding. Men are the same way: possessive, obsessive and cruel. But I felt she was this lonely intelligent girl that I was getting to know at my own sluggish pace. The sight of her with this guy, whoever he was, bothered me.

As a result, she avoided me whenever she came into the library. Several times she couldn't because I was the only check out person, which was when she would be civil but rushed. I found myself still very interested in what books and audio recordings she was exploring, so I would, when no one else was around, go into the system - I had the Administrator Password form when I worked with Bradley, who never changed it - and found out her personal information like home address and personal phone number, which I took home with me.

I was in my bedroom, bored, everyone was off elsewhere in the house doing their own thing, and so I got a hold of the family camcorder, put in a blank cassette, and started fooling around, recording myself dancing and jumping around and making faces at the camera. At one point, I started to strip. That's when I got a crude idea: I set up the camera to face the blank white wall in my room and sit it on its tripod so that the device was at about waist level. I stood in front of it and began pleasuring myself. I've seen things like that in adult videos and on the

Internet. I thought it might be fascinating to see myself from an outside perspective. With all these crude home videos you see, it's as if personal video equipment was designed for the act of self-exposure.

When finished, I edited the tape using the camcorder and a VCR to make sure nothing but my lower body was on it, and not me dancing or lip-syncing to an imaginary song in my head, stuffed it a padded envelope and mailed it to her home address. I was cautious in how I did it: I went to a public mailbox far away from my house and work, I printed the label at home instead of hand-writing it and stole the stamps from the drawer at the library. I covered my tracks as best as possible.

The following Wednesday I saw her and played civil and polite - I smiled as I scanned her items. I tried to get a sense of how she was looking at me - did she know? Could she tell? She spoke nothing of any mail-delivered gifts, and only remarked that she thought it was unbearably cold outside. After she left, I double-checked the address in the database to make sure it was hers and that I couldn't have sent it to someone else. I looked. It was correct.

Amazingly, nothing ever happened. Nothing was ever said.

I tried looking at her whenever she came in to see what she was thinking or feeling. Did she suspect me? Did she watch the tape? When she stood right in front of me my pulse raced feverishly and I began to sweat in panic. What if she hit me? I would sit in my room upstairs and feel my heart skip when the doorbell rang downstairs, fearing it would be the police or Federal Bureau of Investigation.

Every subsequent time I saw her, she - and I truly believe this - looked a little more worn out. Sad, tired, I'm not sure. We never spoke at length about anything of substance any more. Maybe the pressures of home and relationships were taxing her. I never saw her Rob again. I don't think she ever thought it was me, or else, why continue talking to me?

Part of me, later, felt a quiet thrill and other part felt small and pathetic. What did I want from her, I would think to myself as I tried to sleep? I think I wanted to see a change in her and I wanted to see that I could bring forth the change. I only did it twice ... or was it three times ... (*Pause*) ... no it was twice, but twice was too many. I miss not knowing what she was reading or watching or listening to, and having to create my own syllabus has not been easy. If and when I marry, if any woman would have me, I would love the person I marry to have a Faustian *need to know*.

19.

Dallas was a city made of glass, shimmering and delicate, hot and uninhabitable. Both it and its shining architecture could be seen from the rabid highway in and around it - a fortress of see-through crystal reflecting the clouds, the ground and the traffic swirling through the highway. Aesthetically, it's a charming wonderment, as if its designers saw it fit to keep the aquatic plainness of the sky uninterrupted and unending - the mirrored windows and angles of the clear, geometrical buildings had a wallflower-ish appeal, as if the people encased in the glass structures did not want to appear big and tall and did not wish to hinder your view of the expanse of blue and white.

The tractor-trailer floated by the clear form, moving with the now-compact school of cars and trucks that had been moving right along with them but were prepared to leave the course and merge with the inner city itself. Amelia nibbled on pieces of pineapple from a plastic container she bought at the gas/food station. She, nor Cameron, were talking much, still balancing - in their mind - what they felt of Marcel's digression and whether or not he was actually lying to them. Keeping with the rough timeline of the stories, Amelia confessed to a particularly low moment:

THE FRIENDS OF AMELIA'S ADULTHOOD

AMELIA: My friend Joanne was getting married - this was a year ago - and a bunch of my friends and I decided that we were going to have this Bachelorette Party for *her* - to go out, get drunk, dance, you know, have a blast. This was partially because her fiancé and his friends were putting on this big weekend-long binge of Paintball and chicanery together and who-knows-what-else, and they were all staying in his one friend's house who was divorced but a little older but lived on an enormous tract of land and going ape. Joanne didn't like this one bit, but he demanded that he get his way, so she told him she was going to get *her* way, and that she was doing the same thing. He begrudgingly said "fine," she begrudgingly said "fine" and the plans were in motion.

Someone suggested we get a stripper to come over but no one could agree on whose apartment he would go to and that idea got nixed. So it was decided that we would dress up in some cheap bridal costumes and all eleven of us - that's with me included - would leapfrog from bar to bar, club to club, paying whatever cover we needed to and going all night.

The issue of driving was never resolved, as I would find out a little later. I suggested that we get a limousine but everyone flinched at the price. It did not end up in my favor, naturally - I ended up as one of the chauffeurs, voted on by everyone but me. They knew I didn't want to do it but they made me anyway - they were quick with the reasoning as well ("We always drive so now it's your turn," and "You don't drink that much anyway," and "So-and-so can't drive because she has points on her Driver's License for speeding whereas you have a clean record"). To "sweeten" the deal, I would have to use my own car, because it simply wasn't big enough to seat as many as Joanne's cousin's SUV.

They lined up the itinerary, they acquired the traditional white, bloated bridal outfits at some costume shop that they paid for without asking me for a cent, they decided who went in what vehicle, and I steered my group from place to place. I kept my alcohol intake low while they pirouetted all around me in their own gowns and lace and blood red eyes, and I switched to cranberry club soda when I just wanted a glass in front of me.

At the third place we got to, I felt in control and amused by Joanne and everyone else's efforts to be the center of attention. I watched from the table I was at as they marched around the patrons, laughing and drawing all available eyes and faces in their direction. The bartenders and waiters and waitresses were all delighted by the production and most clapped them on. At one point, one of Joanne's friend that I didn't know - she was from out of state - asked me for the keys to the car because she said she forgot something in there. I gave them to her and she went outside. Minutes went by, and Joanne and another friend, Renée, brought over this guy, Dennis, who said he wanted to meet me. He sat down and gave me his schpiel - he worked here, did this, did that, asked about me, what was going on, yeah he heard … the usual. He offered to buy me a drink. I said, no I'm taking it easy, so he told me he'd get me a rum and coke with only a "little bit of rum" which I said wouldn't hurt.

Two drinks later - both Dennis' treat - he's talking about his Sister who's making a killing doing real estate in Massachusetts, and I looked up and saw that the other girls were gone. I got a little nervous, stood up and woozily stomped outside. Dennis followed me. I looked in the parking lot. "They left without you," he observed correctly. I was enraged, beside myself. "Why did they do that?" I asked aloud. "Let's sit down and wait, maybe they'll come back," he said.

We sat down and talked about what might have happened. I kept my eye on the rest of the room to see if they were all crunched in the bathroom or something absurd like that. I stupidly kept my purse in the SUV with my cell phone so I couldn't call them, and the bartender told me I couldn't use the bar phone, and the pay phone was "out of order." Dennis lent me his, which I used but to no avail, and I kept getting voice messages saying the phones were not turned on and would I like to leave a message. I could have cried. I got up to ask the bartender to call a cab for me, which he did. I was so out of sorts, I didn't even think to call one of you.

Dennis intervened. "How are you going to pay for the cab? You don't have your purse." I said we'd work something out. It was at that point he offered to drive me home. He asked for directions and I gave them. "I know where that is, it's not out of the way," he told me. So, we left. I wasn't watching where he was heading at first because I was upset and distracted, but when I came to I realized we weren't going in the direction I stipulated. When I demanded he tell me where he was taking me, he said, "My place for a quick second." Then he didn't say anything for a bit, and followed that with, "Did I tell you that you look great in that wedding dress? All of you do. It's a cool idea." I got testy and told him I didn't want to go to his place. He then got into Placate Mode and was using whatever sincerity and suaveness he had in him to make excuses and sugar coat things.

When we pulled into the driveway of this house he told me he'd make me coffee and it's no big deal, after the coffee he would be happy to take me home. I got much louder with him. He told me to be calm, be calm, we'd sit, talk, and "that was it." I did get out of the car and head inside, but I was really intending to use the house phone to get someone to pick me up. Inside, I sat at the kitchen table and he honestly did put on a pot of coffee ("Decaf vanilla almond work for you?"). I didn't ask to use the phone - I just went over to it and picked up the receiver. I tried to call a few people, including Joanne, but it did no good. He got very close to me when he handed me my mug. I told him when I finished my coffee we had to leave. He agreed, poured himself a cup, and then sat directly next to me at the table. He told me I should be careful not to spill the coffee on the white gown. He also told me that he wanted to kiss me. I told him it wasn't a good time, and then he became a little grabby and was rubbing his hand against the lace running along my arm, which I reacted to by jumping up, knocking the coffee mug off the table, knocking over the chair and the ceramic jar in the middle of the table, which then rolled off before he could catch it and smashed on the floor. It made a lot of noise in a very quiet house. Dennis immediately reacted by whispering for me to settle down and ran for paper towels to clean up the coffee and a garbage can to collect the ceramic fragments.

I heard movement and footsteps from the floor above us. I looked around the bend in the darkened house to see who was there. Before I knew it, two people, a man and a woman, in their sixties, stormed into the kitchen with their bathrobes on. The woman spoke first: "What is going on? We're sleeping and it's almost three o'clock in the morning." Before Dennis could speak, the woman looked at me in shock. "Oh my God. Dennis! Did you...." Dennis attempted to interrupt her by saying we were both leaving. But she kept going on. "... Did you steal someone's bride?" she asked. He made efforts to explain the situation, how it was a joke, but his parents kept looking at me. "What joke?" I heard Dennis' father say. I smiled a little, but tried not to make a sound. Dennis explained that he'd clean up the spill and ceramic jar much later, that he was sorry, that he'd go into more detail later, and then grabbed my hand and pulled me out the front door.

This time he did take me home, and the drive was obviously awkward. Part of me wanted to laugh out loud and another just wanted to sit there, somber, but the two of them cancelled each other out and I was able to focus, with one eye shut, on the lights along the highway and the lit buildings and street posts in the far distance. I wanted to get the gown off, because it was too tight up top and I was tired of fidgeting with it. When I got to my apartment, he let me out and the instant I shut the door behind me he took off in a mad hurry.

I realized I didn't have my key so I knocked on the door of my neighbor who had a copy I lent her in case of something like this. She was awake, luckily, since she said she had trouble sleeping and spent the night hours flipping channels. She didn't ask about my get-up and I promised to get into more detail later. She smiled and closed her door.

The following day I paid Joanne an enraged visit and demanded an immediate explanation. I started hollering at her the moment I looked right at her. She was caught off guard and defensive, and seemed confused by my hostility. She said it was all "Renée's idea," that Renée worked with this Dennis character, that the two of us would "hit it off" and that Dennis was a very nice guy who could take me home if need be. She made it sound like she and Renée were doing me a favor, saying they both noticed I was "depressed," which no one else I knew ever told me and that I never felt myself. She said I hadn't been out with anyone for a couple of months and that Dennis needed someone to fix him up. I told her that I needed time off after my previous relationship, which ended poorly as she very well knew. Joanne became irritated because I confronted her like that, and we stopped talking. I couldn't believe they would abandon me with someone like that. I did get my purse back in exchange for the costume, though, and haven't spoken to Joanne since.

CAMERON: I remember you talking about that guy you dated for a while. Didn't you say he was possessive?
AMELIA: Griffin? (*Scoffs*) He made me wear a pager so he could contact me at any time. I didn't think anything of it when he first handed it to me, but then he would page me at all hours, ask me who I was with … that, that whole thing was just a mess.

CAMERON: Did you ever see Darren again?

AMELIA: No. But the episode I had was very close to an episode my Grandmother once told me about. She was going roller-skating at this place called the SkateAway with her friend Hannah and their dates. She was almost sixteen or seventeen, and this was the 1940's. Hannah and her boyfriend got out of the car to go into the park behind the SkateAway where everyone, she said, "made out." She was left in the front seat with her date, who she said was a little older than her. The way she tells it, before they even *went* skating he lunged at her, groping and being very ungentlemanly, and she kept pushing back and trying to get away. She pushed so hard against the door to get away from him that it popped open and she tumbled backwards and landed on her head. She was cut so badly her date had to take her to get stitches. But she told me that despite the headache and bleeding and stitches, she was glad it happened, and assured me with the utmost conviction that she prayed for the door to open and it did just that.

20.

At the Scabbard Inn in Western Texas where the Troupe spent the night, Cameron slept on a cot that was folded up in the corner while Amelia took the bed on the right and Marcel the one closest to the air conditioner. He woke up at 5:30, frozen and shaking. He stomped over to the air conditioner to adjust the dials to the "low" position without shutting off the device completely. He also thought about the dream that was interrupted:

THE DREAM OF THE PLASTIC BOAT

CAMERON: A group of people I never met before and I were playing on a beach with Frisbees and beach balls and volleyballs - a small dog was following the objects as they soared directly above him. But I grew bored, and wandered off down the coast, where I spotted a boat made of plastic and rubber, docked along the shoreline. The passengers on the boat were wearing SCUBA gear and noticeably rushed as they scrambled around, looking busy; one of the men standing by told me I had to get on the vessel as fast as possible. As we sailed along, I saw the water swell violently around the boat, and the water's color went from tropical translucent blue-green to a thick purple. I noticed that the people on board, noticed the thickening, cannibalistic water, became visibly panicked and uncontrollably frightened, and in sequence hurled themselves off the side of the boat and into the viscous fluid to get free, to escape from the boat they were on with me. But I stayed, comforted by the beauty of the vibrant glow and eased by the non-threatening sky. The boat was not heading in any particular direction, and thinking back, I should have been worried because everyone else seemed to be, but the enormity of the rapidly transforming, coagulating water and the warm wind did not bother me at all.

21.

Amelia and Cameron asked Marcel about why he wanted to go to Santa Fe so badly, when it was so out of the way, and he said that he remembered when he was delivering dentures that the secretary he worked with closely had kept postcards and mementos of places she visited all over the world and liked to keep those little trinkets and bobbles around her desk. She was a certified travel junkie - and Marcel suspected her husband (who was not the dentist) had a very high-paying job with an excess of time off - who lived in countless cities and places and always felt the compulsion to pack up and go. Among those items he could remember: a photo of the beach at La Jolla, a large boat in Montreal, some snapshots of Rio, another outside the Parthenon and one of a pueblo in Santa Fe. He didn't remember what she said about any of those places other than "It was *so* wonderful" but her enthusiasm was genuine. It was as if the enormity and exoticism of each place was too much for her to bother describing, as if the thoughts she had of them were too private and personal to share.

Cameron, who had traveled to Las Vegas with a group of his friends for a five-day excursion was reminded of some stories he took away from there:

THE NIGHT IN THE GARDEN

CAMERON: The flights, at the time, were ridiculously cheap, so a whole bunch of us - my two cousins and three friends from Illinois you've never met - all flew out there and met up for this package deal that was engineered by the Illinois group. My friends met my cousins a couple of times before and they got along marvelously with each other, so it wasn't a problem. We stayed at the Luxor together - the six of us drew lots and stuffed ourselves into whichever room we wound up getting. We gambled, woke up early, took caffeine tablets to stay awake. Most people, we noticed, slept late because of the hot hot heat, got dressed up around 4 PM and then switched back and forth along the Vegas Strip, travelling from casino to casino, trying the different tables, and then later on, went dancing in whatever club was most popular and that they could finagle their way into. We were in too much of a hurry to sleep the morning away, so that's when we piled into a rental car and drove to Red Rocks to climb around the almost Martian-like terrain and cruise around the outskirts of the city - the less glamorous side.

The second night we were there - a Friday - all six of us went to a place called the VIP Lounge, a Gentleman's Club. Instead of taking a taxi, all three walked it using some vague directions on a water park brochure someone wrote down in the margin. My friends gave my cousins every chance to back out, but everyone was geared to go, including me.

The fee to get in was only $10 a piece, and we were told that that included one and only one non-alcoholic drink. When we went in, there were dozens of empty chairs circling the stage, a couple sitting next to the stage on the left, two guys alone in a corner and an older man somewhere in the middle of the room. We took our seats and stared at the stage, aglow with beams of light and the only lit spot in an otherwise darkened room. The music kicked in, and from behind the lime-colored curtain emerged a shapely blonde with high-heels and a nurse's outfit barely on - a classical dress-up role for couples and something of a cliché. She posed, kicked, spun and flipped while clothing slowly came off: the shoes, the white gloves, the hat, the half-buttoned top, the tight shirt, the thong. She pressed against the pole emerging from the end of the stage and slithered and turned - she grabbed a hold of the pole and contorted herself in such a way that Robert - a cousin - had to clap. The couple next to the stage was clapping, too, and threw a few bills on the corner of the stage. The woman on the stage picked them up without making it obvious, made a few bending gestures for the couple, who continued clapping, and afterwards went off stage after grabbing her discarded clothing.

Following that ... there was nothing. Two girls from out of nowhere came over to us and asked if we wanted drinks. I said no and Warren - a friend; he was next to me - also said no. I was then talking to Warren about something or other, and the same two girls came back with what appeared to be bright red cups and were handing them to the two of us. I told her I didn't want it. She said, "You paid for it. It's just club soda." She also handed a cup to Warren, who learned from my example and just accepted the cup.

We sipped our sodas and sat anxiously awaiting another girl on stage, but out of some side doors appeared more of the dancers - a few of them had bras on, some did not. The girls paraded in front of us, asking each and every one of us if we wanted 'a dance.' This meant you go into the back room with a girl - the back room was called The Garden, harmoniously enough - and back there the girl would dance for you for the duration of one song - a private dance where the gyrations on stage would become much more personal. It sounded tempting, but I was nervous and uncomfortable, so I kept turning the girls down, opting to stay in my seat and continue watching the routines on the stage. Benjamin - a friend - caught sight of a girl he was particularly interested in - she was a tall brunette with a pom-pom cheerleader novelty bra on, and when she made her way over to us, he practically fell over himself telling her "yes, I do want a dance." I thought he made a wise choice - I would have gone with her if I had the courage. Edmond - a friend - left to go with the thin Asian girl who was visibly angry when Warren declined her second invitation to a dance, after which he turned to me, unnerved, and whispered, "What did I do?" to which I shrugged - and Samuel - a cousin - took off with a spindly blonde who reminded him of both Brittany Murphy and Farrah Fawcett.

Warren and I were left alone, then, in the main room while the rest of my friends and cousins were off - I told him I wasn't going back there and Warren did too, placing the blame on his (then) girlfriend who he was seeing for a couple of weeks and "wouldn't want to lie to." I told him I would never tell her if he did go back just once, but he said he'd "stay loyal." I rolled my eyes but also liked the fact that I wasn't the only person there actually drinking the free drink.

A few shows went on stage, and it was like a movie to me: there were slow stretches where anticipation built up, waiting to see the next girl disrobe completely and then the next one and the next one and the next one, and with each girl came a different theme, and with the theme came the appropriate costume, song, and dance that fit the beat of the song. One girl played this heavy metal song while slowly removing the leather and fish net stocking and black boots - she would play-growl and play-snarl from time to time and clench her fists. Another had angel wings that flapped when she pulled a cord, and a halo made of tinsel. Yet another was a schoolgirl, with the Catholic Teenager ensemble of plaid skirt, sweater, non-prescription glasses and pigtails. Every dancer needed a gimmick.

In a short period of time after their departure to the back room, Samuel and Edmond came back to their seats minutes apart. Robert emerged a few minutes after them. Warren and I learned over to them to ask how it was, and each one was beaming. "Are you going back?" Warren asked. "If I had more money," Sam told us. Warren and I offered to put our remaining cash together for him. When I handed it all to him, he waved me off saying, "Nah, I'm good," and turned his enthusiasm towards the main stage.

Girl after girl appeared on the stage or in front of us, asking for money (indirectly). "Once is enough," Edmond said over and over, and with a laugh. The girls did not stop coming by. They kept asking and asking. The place never gathered any new customers, and the few people that were already there when we arrived were getting ready to leave. While sitting there, the five of us waited for

Benjamin, who was still in the back. We looked around the room - Samuel offered to go outside to look, thinking he was waiting out there for us. Nothing. Sam went over to one of the bouncers behind the counter with the soda dispensers. He came back to us. "He's not outside. The guy over there says he's still in The Garden." We kept on waiting.

An hour and forty-five minutes later - we timed - he emerged, hair mussed and clothing slightly disheveled. We said we were ready to leave, and further, what the hell happened? He grinned and shrugged playfully. Outside, all of us badgered him about the girl with the pom pom bra. He told us to be quiet - he was feeling good and just wanted to remain quiet for a little while. To make up for his silence, Edmond told us about the girl he was with - she told him her name was "Krystal" with a "K" - said that the girls were all disappointed by the night's poor turn out, so we'd probably be "hounded" to have more private dances than usual. Krystal told him that the private dances were how they made the majority of their money, and with no customers, no tips.

We went straight to bed - it was my night to actually get one of the beds, like we'd worked out earlier, and it was Ben's turn to sleep on the inflatable floor mattress. Well, he wanted the bed. Warren refused to give his up, so he tried reasoning with me. He told me that if I gave it to him, he'd buy me breakfast, lunch *and* tell me what happened. I agreed.

The following day he did pay for my coffee and French Toast - the others were off gambling and the two of us were smoking the Dunhill cigars he brought from home. He told me that everything started out smoothly - they went into the back, which had different rooms all lined up and with curtains, and she instructed him to take his shoes off, lay on the bed, to put his feet up and to stop looking at her. She got on top of him, twisted, writhed, ran her hands along his arms and chest. The rule is that the patron is not allowed to touch the girl, but the girl can touch the patron. When her one song was over, he was expecting her to get up. But she stayed on him. "Would you like me to keep going?" she asked. He shook his head yes. He went through all she did - rubbing her breasts in his face, sliding her G-string around so her privates were exposed and rubbing herself along his shirt and the side of his face. Then she talked to him for a little bit, about how a lot of the girls are actually homosexuals, just the way a significant percentage of male dancers are, how she's using the money to support her son, how any dancer that tells you she's going to college is most likely a liar, how cruel the business of doing what she does can be.

She then started back up again, after what Ben jokingly claimed was their "time to bond," and asked all these playful porn-script questions like "how bad are you?" and "how bad do you want me to be?" She laughed and he said he laughed and he felt that she was as aware of the idiocy of the statements as he was. Then, she slid his belt out of his pants after unfastening it with her free hand - her other hand was tussling his hair - slowly pulled it from underneath him and smacked his side with it lightly, then his legs, then his arms - they got progressively harder, to the point where the crack was audible. When I asked him why he didn't tell her to stop, he said he was laughing too hard, and she looked like she was enjoying it.

The real hit came when he eventually left the back room and his dancer gave him his bill: $540. Shocked but not wanting to offend her, he gave his credit card, thanked her for everything, and she told him to please come back because he was one of her "best customers." He was on such a high that the cost of the experience didn't really *really* sink in until later, when he panicked and worried his fiancé would see the charge on his credit card. But he shrugged it off and said he'd worry about the bill when he got home. He said the thrill of being touched by someone new, and not having to touch them, was worth the price, if you thought about it.

THE EXTRAVAGANT FAMILY

CAMERON: Since it was cumbersome to always travel in a pack of six, we often split up and went our separate ways with the intention of meeting up later. I wanted to slum around the older parts of Vegas, in the junk shops and go to the video game arcade in Circus-Circus and so did Robert and Ben, while the others wanted to hang around the $5 blackjack tables and actually, consciously, try to make some money - enough to pay for the room and flight for all of us. Though realistically pessimistic, they were determined. While I played blackjack for a while - and some craps - it couldn't hold my interest for that long.

We met up later for a show Sam scammed someone out of six tickets for, a midnight Vegas spectacular called "Night Time Pleasures," which was your usual tits and smoke affair. It had poor production qualities and the room was small and cramped - like a grindhouse theater that was showing *The Opening of Misty Beethoven* - but it offered nothing more than innocuous entertainment and we left feeling lighthearted.

Earlier, though, while my group was drinking quarter beers and eating dollar hot dogs and looking for oddities in the casinos and five and dime stores, Sam, Edmond and Warren were a few miles away having a glamorous meal at an upscale restaurant built into the casino called Indigo that Edmond wanted to try. They told us their story while we were walking back to our rooms at the end of the night:

The three of them sat at a table in the left-most corner of the snug room, one table down and one across from them sat an older man next to a much younger woman and at the other side of the table, an older woman who was probably his wife. Sam and Warren were facing the man and girl so they had an excellent view of the activity - Edmond's back was turned and he didn't want to make any obvious moves. While they were waiting for their meals, Sam and Warren watched the family across from them with deep focus and intensity. The girl had to be in her early twenties while the man and woman were both well over sixty. There was something off about them, maybe in the way the old man kept patting the girl's hand every once in a while, maybe in the way they looked like they didn't know each other. Samuel, too, thought the girl was exceptionally pretty, which added to the level of interest.

When the family's meals were brought to them, Sam and the gang kept looking. The waitress for the family's table was also their waitress, and they followed every single item she brought to them: a carafe of water, straws and extra napkins, small bowls of chilled soup, small dishes of salad. What was perverse was how the old man and woman sat and ate their own meals, but the girl wouldn't touch hers - in between mouthfuls, the old man put his own utensils down and picked up the girl's spoon or the girl's fork and would proceed to feed her - he picked at the lettuce and brought some greens to her mouth, he carefully dipped the spoon into the soup for her to sip on. After some salad and some soup he lifted the glass of water he poured for her from the carafe and put a straw in for her to drink from. Both Samuel and Warren were whispering to Edmond what was happening, while Edward examined their faces for shifts in expression. "Now what are they doing?" he'd ask sporadically, only to be answered in due time by the two sentinels. The older woman, it seemed, wasn't taking part in the feeding, but sat and ate and watched herself. "Is the girl handicapped?" Edmond asked. "Not a clue," Warren responded.

Their waitress, in the middle of all this, appeared suddenly, catching the three of them by surprise. She brought their meals and told them to "Enjoy," and winked as she walked away. All three ate their meals but the two kept peering up from their plates to see what was happening next. Come dessert time, they saw that it was the old woman's turn to delicately cut and feed the girl chocolate cake. When they were finished eating cake, the old man wiped the girl's mouth with a napkin. Shortly thereafter, they paid and left, while Samuel, Warren and Edmond stuck around for crème brûlée and coffee and gin and tonics and the rest of the restaurant slowly emptied out to more reasonable proportions.

At 10, they were still sitting there, adding to the already ghastly dinner bill that their blackjack earnings couldn't even cover, and it was the end of their waitress' shift and they wanted to give her the tip in person. Unexpectedly, with baseball hat on and handbag slung around her shoulder, she stopped by the table to sit down and chat and ask where they were from and offer a little bit about herself. "I see you noticed that table," she said as she was sitting down in the fourth seat at the table. "Isn't that something?" Samuel nodded. "It's a shame, she's so pretty but she looks ... disabled or mentally retarded." The waitress roared. "Disabled? Christ, no, she's not disabled." Samuel didn't flinch. "Okay, so what's going on then?"

The waitress told them that the girl was an escort hired by the old man and woman for the night. She'd seen the girl in there before with different men and a few women. She said she would come in alone to eat sometimes and they got to know each other a little bit. As an escort, people can ask for different things, certain types of individuals, with certain physical features, and from what the waitress gathered, the elderly couple hired the girl to be their daughter for the evening, which may explain why they were doting on her in that way. In the past, the escort said the people she'd been with had bought outrageously expensive items for her, like dresses, watches and bracelets and dressed her up for the evening with specific clothes *they* picked out and stipulated how she must wear her hair, what accessories to wear and so on. She got compensated well for going with these people and playing the roles they gave her. Someone, one time, needed her to be his wife for the night, and on another occasion she had to be this one person's best friend from childhood or maybe even just a plain old girlfriend. She plays the part, no questions asked, the waitress said, and everyone is pleased.

The three guys hearing this couldn't believe it. They offered to buy their waitress a drink in some other establishment to continue their conversation, but she said she had a "pressing engagement elsewhere" and needed to leave immediately. Once she left, they left too, and when they walked off they went to continue playing blackjack, since the meal had them in the hole.

22.

The Troupe arrived in hot, earth tone Santa Fe at 2 PM, close to the same time they found themselves in New Orleans days earlier. Navigating the crowded, multi-lane roads cutting through the horizontal city was challenging for Marcel, who just wanted to get a hotel room and get on with his plans for the town. They searched for - and found - four different hotels to stay at, but all had No Vacancy, and they were getting impatient. They asked the clerk at the fourth hotel they stopped in for a directory guide and wanted to know where there was a Vacancy, and if he could help them call around to find a room. He agreed out of kindness and part boredom, made a few calls to places he thought would have rooms, and found one that was "relatively inexpensive" and not that far from the downtown area. They thanked him and followed his directions to the Hackman Hotel.

Once they settled in and Cameron was able to go into the bathroom, Amelia fell onto the bed and was staring at the ceiling.

AMELIA: I was looking at the Custom Travel Booklet in the tractor-trailer. If we had stayed on 10 West we would have gotten there much faster. This way is zigzagging around and out of the way. *Why* did we come here again?

MARCEL: First off, it wouldn't have been *that* much shorter. Second, now we get to see this place, which we wouldn't have seen otherwise.

AMELIA: What's here to see?

MARCEL: I have three places I must go to, then it just doesn't matter. Well, technically four, but I'm not sure how to get to the fourth place.

Cameron walked out of the bathroom.

MARCEL: Hey, guess who's buried nearby?

CAMERON: (*Repeating*) Nearby here, nearby, nearby … (*Pause*) I'm not sure what you're saying.

MARCEL: Do you remember which of your favorite authors used to live around here?

CAMERON: (*Thinking*) In Santa Fe?

MARCEL: Well, close by.

CAMERON: (*Shaking his head*) I'm drawing a blank.

MARCEL: D… (*Pause*) H…

CAMERON: (*Ah-ha*) D. H. Lawrence! That's right! He died … no, he died elsewhere, but it was reported that they shipped, like, his ashes back here, didn't they?

MARCEL: Well, we should look for the memorial or whatever they set up here if we have time.

CAMERON: *We have to hate our immediate predecessors to get free of their authority.*

AMELIA: Do you want to do it now?

MARCEL: Not without a rental car. I planned to use it for only a day and jet out of here, so….

AMELIA: It's 3 PM. (*Pause*) Is the day shot?

MARCEL: I say we postpone traveling to these places until tomorrow. We can get everything done tomorrow. If we can't, well, that's it. We'll leave the next day for San Diego.

Amelia got up and gathered some cash and all three of them walked out towards town for some light sightseeing. They picked up a brochure in the hotel lobby to see where the "hot spots" were and wanted to get to as many as they could before closing time. They also asked the clerk how far it would be to walk to the downtown, and she told them it was about a mile, maybe a little more. They decided to hike it.

While walking, Amelia thought it would be a good time to call home and talk to her parents, and Cameron opted to do the same. Marcel walked along side both of them, looking up and around at the tan-colored mock-primitive buildings, crafted and aligned with careful aesthetic precision. He thought about borrowing one of their phones to call Lucile, to hear how she was doing, how everyone was feeling, but didn't dare, and imagined everyone was fine.

They turned in early that night, in lieu of a busy following day, and before they went to bed Amelia called the main desk to rent a Jeep for them to do some local driving (Cameron was the one who spotted the sign in the lobby that said, "Let us get you your rental vehicle!"). After gobbling down some of the stale complimentary breakfast (dry cereal, bagels) the next morning and getting directions from the front desk to three places Marcel wanted to visit - the woman at the desk, who was still working the next morning, never heard of D. H. Lawrence's grave - they picked up the rental Jeep right outside the hotel lobby (delivery of the automobile was also complimentary and convenient - they were to leave it in the same spot when they finished and give the keys to the front desk. Easy!)

1. Tesuque Pueblo.

The hotel worker said that the Taos Pueblo was the most popular Pueblo, she recommended this Pueblo as an alternative, which she said she visited regularly for some of their special events. Marcel volunteered to drive there since it was his idea to do all of this extra stuff, but Cameron refused and took the keys. Marcel relented, but demanded he sit in the passenger seat. Amelia let him go, all too pleased to get in the backseat to stretch out. It was a pleasant day and they had sunscreen, so before they left, Marcel and Cameron took the roof off the Jeep. After so long in the compressed cabin of the tractor-trailer, it was a pleasant thrill to have the air fully circulating again.

They arrived at the Pueblo early and were worried it wasn't open - they parked the Jeep in the assigned but vacant lot and walked towards the main entrance building at the very front. It was locked, so they knocked, and soon a middle-aged man with tinted glasses came to the door. He told them the place was open but since it was the middle of the week and early it was very empty. They paid a nominal fee for the upkeep of the Pueblo and were given small maps of the village to give themselves a clue as to where to go. He told them that they came at a bad time if they wanted a full tour and wanted to witness some of the dancing and what he called "touristy" things, but they told him they were passing through, and all that was not necessary.

No signs of life existed in the orderly but dusty village - several shops were open that sold Kachina dolls - statues of American Indian gods/spirits - along with turquoise jewelry, bags, pottery and t-shirts that had the name of the Pueblo on it and below the name some symbols for the rain, the sun and lightning or a picture of the ubiquitous Kokopelli, the fertility god.

Back outside, two children were playing with sticks - a little boy and a little girl. The boy was older than the girl, but not by much. As Marcel, Amelia and Cameron passed by them, the little girl - who was an Albino, and whose face was visibly damaged and hauntingly translucent - used the stick she was playing with and went up to Cameron and rubbed it against his right arm. All three stopped to see what she wanted, but she just looked at him, then turned around and ran back towards the boy she was with who watched her from a safe distance. Amelia looked at Cameron strangely and asked why she did that to him. Cameron, a little unnerved, wondered if it was some kind of greeting, or if the girl was mad they were there. He kept watching the two kids as they went inside one of the nearby houses.

They saw less and less as they walked, and a growing unease formed when Marcel voiced his opinion that he felt like he was tromping through someone's front yard or neighborhood, that the people of the Pueblo - while eager to let the public witness how their ancestors lived - were engaging in an act of borderline self-exploitation, and that intruding, although inexplicably welcomed, was still odd. It's like a house tour that's being put on for charity where you pace through people's hallways to admire how they dolled each and every room up, and all the while the house's inhabitants are humming to themselves and cooking eggs in the kitchen while the stereo plays softly in the next room.

What made that feeling worse was the lack of residents outside or tourists snapping photographs to add to the sense of being a part of a friendly, visiting community. After covering only a third of the "key points" marked on the Tesuque Pueblo map, Cameron drove to destination two.

2. The Santuario de Chímayó.

A small chapel that Marcel heard about when researching the Action, this was a place that was reputed to have "sacred dirt," which some claimed had healing powers. The parking area for this site was packed, and so was the path into the Sanctuary. The Troupe nudged their way into the funnel of people and step by step got closer to the entrance.

The inside was dark and cramped with people of all races and ages, taking photographs of the walls and signs. The three of them squeezed their way into the room with the soil, which had men and women and children pulling out of the hole in the ground and stuffing into tiny jars they brought with them - pill boxes, plastic bags, empty juice containers. Marcel ducked and twisted to work his way towards the hole in the center of the room, knelt down and grabbed fistfuls of dirt, which he pushed into the pockets of his shorts.

Marcel caught sight of Amelia outside the door to that room and asked if she had any containers of her own, and after a quick sifting through her purse, said she didn't. She was reading, in the long passageway out, one of the innumerable letters of people who said that the sanctuary cured them. The room itself was so bizarre and fascinating it could not be forgotten: crutches, braces, makeshift crosses, drawings, poems, dirty Polaroids, stories - all lined up along the wall, left by visitors, and on full display for the curious.

Back in the car, Marcel grabbed clumps of the dirt from his pockets and put some of it in the ashtray so it didn't fall out of his pockets and he could safely store it later on. Cameron found a plastic bag in the glove compartment where he put the rest. Noticing that his hands were covered with crumbs and pieces and he had nothing to wash them with, Marcel rubbed his fingers and palms over his face and into his thick, dry hair.

3. Taos.

Deciding not to bother with the Taos Pueblo after the unpleasant feelings gathered from Tesuque, they headed to downtown Taos, which was a lovely and erudite little hamlet, low and hot and populated with numerous tourist types and a marked shortage of parking spaces for all of them. Not yet tired, they parked at a meter far from the center of town, put change into it so they could remain at the space for three hours and took their merry time strolling around. Families with strollers, teenagers, elderly couples and children moved up and down the dolled-up blocks, taking their own sweet time, looking in every window and shop.

Amelia remarked how the town seemed a lot like parts of the French Quarter - and places beyond the French Quarter - in New Orleans, and, as she thought before, New Hope in Pennsylvania - very moderate-to-up-scale décor, antique shops, many art galleries featuring paintings that attempted to reproduce O'Keeffe but only came across as junk simulacra, Native American paintings, pottery, crafts, clothing, chocolate makers and, as one would expect, outdoor cafes. Even though none of them cared for the arts and crafts of the type that was on display, all three browsed the showroom, not so much out of interest in the craftsmanship but out of a need to step into an air-conditioned room after being exposed to intense afternoon heat.

They stopped in a small restaurant with outside seating, fans and a large green canopy. All ordered light with the intent of eating an early dinner and getting to bed at a reasonable time and leaving the next morning. While sitting and waiting for their meal, they drank their watermelon sodas and conversed with as few words as possible. Marcel and Cameron debated whether or not there was a contradictory message being sent by the village(s) regarding religion - Cameron found it odd in how it's simultaneously commercialized and yet sacred, like the Native American culture itself. They talked about fanaticism.

Amelia was reminded of an incident at her own church while growing up, and offered a small side story to tide them over until their meals arrived.

(Digression)
THE MOVING CHRIST

AMELIA: At our church, our former pastor had retired and a new priest was brought in to fill his place. He was paunchy, bald and breathed heavily, but the breathing wasn't creepy, it just made everyone afraid he was going to pass out during Mass. A new decree was passed at the church that allowed girls to be altar servers - before it was a boys-only thing - so this new priest, Father Anthony, asked my parents if I could help out with the ceremony when they needed me. I agreed and they agreed - remember, this was a couple of years before I stopped going altogether. I was really bored just sitting in the pew and having to listen to the same mass over and over again, but found the idea of helping to run the mass, of being a part of the ceremony, to be a better way to pass the hour.

Rumors were circulating about Father Anthony's former parish and some kind of controversy that took place there. It wasn't discussed in front of me, but since I helped out a few times and talked a little bit with him before and after mass, I really wanted to know. A girl I knew from school went to the same church, and though we didn't know each other very well, I asked her about what little information she had. It seems the church Father Anthony was at was closed down because of strange problems they were having inside the church and the people were getting fanatical. She didn't know why. My Mother feigned ignorance.

So before one of the few masses I was helping with, while in the rectory, standing and waiting for 10:30 mass to begin, I asked him outright about this church. He looked shocked and I was expecting him to get mad. But instead he leaned in close and told me a condensed version. At his previous parish, there was a statue of the crucified Jesus some three to four times the size of an actual man suspended by wires above the altar. He said that during the second Saturday night mass - and there were two, one at 4 PM and another at 7 PM - he stood before the altar and looked above him and something didn't feel right. He said he sensed something was wrong with the statue. When mass was over and everyone left, he went back out to look at the statue. He said that before the skin color of the statue was a gray color, but when he looked again it appeared to be turning brown. He thought he was seeing things, so he went to bed and tried not to think about it. So that night he had trouble sleeping.

Sunday morning, he couldn't stop looking at the statue. He made the mistake of telling someone in the parish what he thought. The two of them kept a close eye on it together. As they would observe the next few days - and they often sat in the front pew for a while looking at it from different angles and seeing the effect of dimmed light or intense light on it - it was not only changing skin tone, but also perspiring. The shell of the statue was slightly moist. He talked to one of the maintenance people who said the moisture could have come from the air-ducts directly above the statue. People didn't care, and hordes of them came with still cameras and video cameras. No one knew what was going on, and Father Anthony said he couldn't control the people and the local media's attention. The end of the story became muddled, but I gather they had to close the parish down because of it.

You could tell by looking at him when he told the story he was bothered by it and wanted to tell me the story: people talk about problems or issues over and over to get it right in their own minds or maybe get input from others as to what they saw. But I didn't have a response for him when he was done with the story except to say, "That's spooky." He shook his head and told me I was absolutely right.

A few months later, I overheard my Mom and her Sister talking about an episode of *Unsolved Mysteries* with Robert Stack that someone got a hold of that had a segment on Father Anthony's former parish. This she let me watch. Everything Robert Stack talked about followed with his version of the events - and then some - and the fact that the church was closed by the diocese was also true. The television show didn't have any answers, my Mom and Aunt didn't, and Father Anthony wasn't sure either, but he did tell me after that particular mass that he was delighted to go to another church and never set foot in that one again. He also liked how our church's statue of Jesus was only five feet high.

23.

They had asked their waitress at that small café where D.
H. Lawrence's grave was, and she said she wasn't sure, so
she brought over the bus boy who she claimed had an idea
but he told them he'd only heard of it and had never been
there. They directed the Troupe to a collectible's store
across the street that sold framed copies of *Look*, *Time* and
Life magazines and were instructed to ask the older
gentleman in there for guidance. The older man knew of it,
but wasn't too good with directions - he scribbled out some
crude map of the area with a pencil on the back of his
business card that he wasn't even sure was accurate.
"You'll have to explore a little," he said and handed them
the paper. "It's not worth it, really," he added, "because
Lawrence's ashes are in England. What's there is just a
memorial."

Lie back and think of England, women were often told.

That night, they found themselves back in their hotel
room around 7 PM, ordered Chinese from a restaurant eons
away that they had severe difficulty finding and picked up
two forty-ounce bottles of malt liquor and a bottle of
Belvedere vodka from a nearby liquor store for the
temporary thrill of it. "I was getting so tired of seeing and
eating Tex-Mex," Amelia groaned, and Cameron and
Marcel agreed. They spent the night holed up, watching
black and white movies on television and went to bed early.

They did, of course, skip the hunt for Mr. Lawrence.
Cameron was the first to say it was no big deal for him.

"He didn't spend a whole lot of time here, anyway," Cameron said. And neither, for that matter, did Cameron.

The tractor-trailer stormed south through New Mexico and onto 10 West to San Diego. Cameron had taken over as navigator with the Custom Travel Booklet because Amelia felt sick to her stomach and didn't want to sleep in the cabin because she thought the darkness and rumbling would make her feel worse. She leaned against Cameron and tried not to look out the window.

The total mileage from Santa Fe to San Diego could, if they took their time, be spread out across two separate days, but Marcel insisted they push on, no matter how long it took, into San Diego. If he became too tired he told Cameron he would have to take over the wheel so he could get some rest - but that was a last resort.

The barest necessities of scenery were, at this point, totally wiped out, and so were the other vehicles - it was a long, arid stretch of grinding through flat muddy treeless homeless land, no billboards, no buildings and the most minimal of signs. What was worse was that the rains would kick up so torrentially that Marcel had trouble seeing the road but couldn't stop the tractor-trailer because he didn't have the time. Of interest in certain spots were stroboscopic flashes of lightning hitting the few hills or open fields around them - it didn't make a noise they could hear, but the flashes were wild and frequent, and the feeling of driving through a storm so massive it filled every fraction of sky added spice to the monotony. Amelia, asleep in fetal position, didn't move. The gloom reminded Cameron of a trip he took to Penn State:

THE ALL-NIGHT ARCADE

CAMERON: My cousin Robert was going to Penn State and invited me up for the weekend to see the PSU versus Ohio State game, do some drinking and hang around campus. I left work early on Friday and drove over myself - unlike this vehicle, I actually have a good sound system in my car so I can listen to music and keep my mind occupied. I got there, ate, went to a gathering at someone's house that was okay but nothing spectacular, got to bed, did the tailgating thing with some students and alumni - you'd be shocked by how old a lot of them were - went to the game and so on.

Again, we ate dinner, walked around campus, Robert tried to find out what was going on by making a few phone calls but nothing was happening, so we ended up at his girlfriend's apartment where we watched the end of *Say Anything*... and afterwards he and I left to go back to his apartment. As we were walking, he suggested we stop in this all-night game arcade place that's a cult hangout spot. I said yeah, sure, why not.

The arcade was this smoky, loud palace of older, archaic video games, new games, kids with clove cigarettes, neo-hipsters with pipes and drunk night lifers who could not sleep. It had this low ceiling and was filled to capacity with game consoles, so there was this very personal feel to it, and no matter what time you went there, Robert told me, there were always groups of people roaming around with quarters.

We each got our own quarters from the dollar-to-change machine in the corner of the first room -

there were two rooms: the first one descended into a room lower than it via a ramp - and trolled the aisles for a good co-op or a fighting game. Robert really wanted to play this one game, this one particular game, but two people were already at it, so we reluctantly had to walk to some other machine he didn't want to play until they left. I can't remember the name of the game we played, but I wasn't very good at it, and he cleaned me out and kept playing after most of my quarters had been used. So I looked up and down the aisles of games to see what else I could play because I didn't want to play that game with him again and didn't want to watch him play alone. Down our aisle of arcade cabinets, three seats away, sat on a stool this lovely young girl who was playing - this I remember - "Galaga" and … just crying like I haven't seen anyone cry before. I mean, she was bawling. Uncontrollably. I couldn't hear the sound coming out of her mouth, but I could see her flushed face and the tears running down it. You know the saying by Herzog about how humans need new images or else they'll die, and well, the sight of her clearly upset and still trying to play this game was an Image for me. I nudged Robert to turn and look, but he was too engrossed to bother. No one around her even *looked* at her. Those that did, if they were in a group, noticed her, then immediately did that non-verbal thing where they looked at each other in the group with this knowing glance and then they all rolled their eyes and scattered. While she was there - and she was there a while - people around her, without acknowledging her or engaging in conversation, just moved out. In a short while, she was sitting there, stranded.

I didn't approach her or talk to her either, and when Robert did lose his game he caught sight of her. He said she probably "broke up with her boyfriend," and then promptly stepped over to the game he really wanted to play the instant he got in the door, which the people that had been playing walked away from. Even as he plunked the quarters in the machine, I kept looking at her. I wanted to hug her, to tell her it was okay, whatever it was, and that I wanted to know what happened. Maybe I could help. But I couldn't move.

I don't know why I remember that. I think, maybe, it's the people that drift by you and are never seen or heard from again that haunt and disturb you so much, much more than the people you do know on a one-to-one basis, because you *need* the narrative around their lives to understand them and make sense of them. When you're only given tiny pieces of them, or very small gestures - like this gorgeous brunette I went to school with that smiled at me once as we were walking away from each other and I never knew why - it stays in your mind forever waiting for you to solve. But it can't be solved.

Amelia woke up and felt better once they stopped at a drug store to grab a few bottles of refrigerated water, bottles of StayAwake caffeine-plus tablets and some generic pills for stomach upset. They ate a light lunch and a light dinner and drank enormous amounts of water. The Weigh Station in Arizona cost them precious time because of what the man said was a "computer glitch" - Marcel anticipated a brisk drive through but felt like he was back in Virginia again, back in the lines and chaos.

As the tractor-trailer moved through Western Arizona, past Sedona and Flagstaff - which Amelia wanted to stop at but Cameron became obstinate over and demanded they forge on and Marcel, for the first time, expressed concern about the fish. This caused Amelia to grumble - she didn't want to go to Santa Fe, she wanted to peruse the New Age-type hot spots and meditation centers out of curiosity. Cameron dismissed Sedona as being 'inane and fatuous' without ever having been there himself. "That is how they showed it on television," he added.

Marcel kept a strong hand on the wheel and ignored requests for Cameron to take over - Marcel felt he was in control; it was his responsibility, he was getting closer to the goal line, he was encroaching the destination. No longer able to read the itinerary in the Custom Travel Booklet, they talked freely and nervously, about romance, about angst, about destitution. Their logorrhea continued.

24.

San Diego, speckled and barely perceptible and virtually inactive, was finally reached somewhere close to three in the morning, and the bliss of being there was diminished by the fatigue and irritability and lack of proper nutrition for the day. All three members of the Troupe were barely conscious and they debated parking the tractor-trailer at some deserted spot and using each others' bodies as pillows to sleep and regain composure. But they followed the signs for the Hotel Circle - an area specifically designated for a long bending snake of hotels, grouped together for convenience. They stopped at the Duvall Hotel, because it was first in line, got the room key, pulled the tractor-trailer to someplace away from the other cars, close to the fence and the outdoor, in-ground swimming pool and shuffled to their room, 211, walked inside, and fell down. Luckily, the beds caught them. Marcel took the one next to the window, as he'd done several times before, and Amelia went for the one farthest from the air conditioner, as she'd done several times before. Cameron fell right next to her, his head on the other pillow.

CAMERON: (*Dazed*) I'm sorry, but I need to sleep in a bed tonight.

AMELIA: (*With eyes closed.*) Oh, I don't care. (*Pause*) Good night.

Marcel, laying on top of the layers of bed sheets, unable and unwilling to move them and cover himself from the blowing streams of frigid air or attempt to get up and lock the room door, just fell asleep. The room light was still on.

At noon the next day, Marcel sat up, startled, and was temporarily disoriented. He calmed down after a couple of seconds, straightened himself out, and stepped outside the door. It was 74°, calm, and with a pure, cloudless sky and even light distributed over all outdoor locations: perfect conditions for a film shoot. Back in the room, Cameron and Amelia were still snuggled together and fast asleep. He used caution not to disturb them, took a quick shower, and realized that his clean clothes were still in the tractor-trailer, so he had to put his ragged clothes back on, sneak past the bed, dart outside, grab one of his travel bags and go back in to get changed. Once finished, he took one of the two room keys, left a note - *Went out to eat be back later* - and walked over to the nearby diner where he ordered the specialty, strawberry waffles and regular coffee. He enjoyed eating alone and not having to look across at anyone or share his booth with someone or hurry up and eat because someone else was in a hurry to leave. After the two men in the booth behind him left, he took the *New York Times* off their table and leafed through it. When he was finished reading, he paid, left a generous tip (26%), washed a handful of pills down with lukewarm coffee and went back to the room.

Amelia was sitting on the corner of the bed watching the local forecast on television.

AMELIA: You took the keys to the tractor-trailer with you and we need our things out of there.

Marcel pulled them out of his pocket and handed them to her.

MARCEL: Want me to get them for you?

AMELIA: That's all right. I'll go.

MARCEL: While you're doing that I'll go to the front desk to rent a car.

He did, and in doing so, found out about some local tourist destinations that were popular, like the San Diego Zoo (an obvious attraction) to the various beaches that were worth spending time on. The clerk gave directions on where a rental car could be obtained - regrettably, the Duvall Hotel was not the Hackman Hotel, and 'didn't deliver' the cars.

Marcel left and went back to the room, where both Amelia and Cameron were sitting at the edge of the bed watching some special report on the bombing of a United States Embassy in Turkey. He told them what the clerk told him, and presented them with some of the swag he was handed - local booklets and keychains and pens. They got up and Marcel drove them to the rental place close to the airport where they grabbed yet another Jeep, same exact model and color as last time. Cameron and Amelia said they needed to go someplace and eat where they could map out what they wanted to see. Marcel told them he wanted none of that - which they suspected earlier - and he said he wanted to drop the tractor-trailer off back at the hotel, be driven to the beach, left there for exactly four hours and picked up much later. Everyone understood, and soon enough he found himself with three hotel towels under him, a mound of dark sand to his immediate left and the sun staring at him from above. Amelia and Cameron wanted to drive to La Jolla, a nearby town, and go shopping and smell the seals lying beached on the rocks for photo opportunities. Marcel, for one small period of time, wanted to do nothing and see nothing, which was exactly what he did.

Lying on the beach in a pair of shorts with his face covered with his polo shirt, he listened to a mixture of waves and children's voices and teenage voices and adult voices and elderly voices, as well as the voices of the feet in the sand, the fists hitting the volleyballs and the hands catching footballs. The sun, he imagined, got closer and closer to him the longer he laid still, and as it got closer and closer the formerly menacing entity became a friendly, understanding compatriot, removing from the sky its infiniteness and leaving only the combination of all colors: white. While thinking, and listening, he dozed off, waking up sporadically to turn over and feel the sweat from his chest slide down both of his sides and around to his back where they were absorbed by the towels beneath him. Occasionally, he'd lift the polo shirt off his face to look upward, flinching, and see a group of teenagers running twenty or thirty feet away from him, playing some kind of game that involved tagging each other and doing handstands.

When he became too warm and feared burning, Marcel put his shirt back on, took one of the towels from under him and draped it over part of his face and didn't move. He was tempted to go look for some cheap food someplace, but he didn't have his wallet on him. He did not want to go into the ocean because he wanted to take some of the time he had alone to walk up and down the pavement parallel with the ocean to get a good idea of the area and its layout and how long it ran. These were all important details to be stored in the registers in his head. He didn't want to stray too far from the spot he was dropped off at for fear of making it a challenge for Amelia and Cameron to find him. But after asking a woman with a sun hat and a dime novel what time it was, he realized he had plenty of leeway to stroll, to examine and to process.

Amelia saw Marcel first, at 5 PM as specified, and she said Cameron was double parked and waiting for them to leave. On the way back to the Jeep she asked:

AMELIA: When do you have to make that delivery of yours? Do you know where to go?

MARCEL: I think so. It's written down in the tractor-trailer. I'll drop it off tonight.

AMELIA: Why tonight? Why not … right now?

MARCEL: It's usually done at night.

AMELIA: (*Nodding*) Ohhhh. Do you need help?

MARCEL: I'll take care of it.

AMELIA: (*Smiling*) I see.
MARCEL: (*Pause*) What?
AMELIA: (*Smiling*) Hmm?
MARCEL: You're ... is something wrong?
AMELIA: (*Shakes head*) Nothing is wrong.

Marcel asked about their couple of hours in La Jolla, and she said it was pleasant, clean and exactly like Santa Fe and Taos and New Orleans and New Hope, with more art galleries, t-shirt shops, quaint antiques and other innocuous tourist temples. He asked her if she saw any theaters and she told him she really didn't look for any.

Later they all ate in the Downtown District at one of the random and rapidly shifting restaurants lined up in a row so completely similar - copious outdoor seating, off white interiors, twentysomething attractive females to seat you and happy with the exposure, green umbrellas at each table, menus remarkably alike (apparently food types can only be 'fused' a certain number of times). Service was slow despite a minimal crowd.

Marcel repeated himself by explaining to Cameron - and Amelia once more - his plans to finally dispense with the fish at night, and that they would need an extra day in San Diego. He asked the two of them how their plans were holding up, and both said that they were spending roughly what they predicted they would - and therefore set aside - for the trip.

After the meal, they did some sidewalk-stomping, window-shopping and people-watching. Cameron bought a small cigar called a "Havana Honey" that came in a plastic container with a plastic bee on it; it was not from Havana - those were too expensive - but it did, he claim, "taste like honey." He nursed the cigar outside while mentally-musing about Castro's death and the soil in Cuba and Amelia and Marcel went in and out of the independent record stores and bought specially-treated drinks from juice bars that you could add extra vitamins and minerals to. Marcel requested Vitamin E, Amelia went with Vitamin A, and when they asked Cameron through the window if he wanted a drink with ginseng or valerian root he made a grouchy face and gave a thumbs down sign.

They returned to the hotel room that night and flipped the television on; Marcel decided there was time to make the delivery and told them he'd be back in a short while. He started up the tractor-trailer with high anxiety and his hands were tremblingly slightly - it was after 1 AM, he was a little tired, his skin a little sunburn and he was trying to remember from earlier on in the day exactly what place he scouted and was going to make the delivery to.

It was the middle of the week and the streets were mercifully bare, the people were inside and industrial buildings had the lights out - except a few floors where cleaners or security guards were prowling. He drove the tractor-trailer slowly at first, keeping an eye on road signs and keeping his fingers crossed that he was going the right way. He wished he'd driven the rental car to and from the beach, since he always remembered directions better when he drove than when he was in the backseat and talking or twirling his head around, examining buildings and pedestrians. He vaguely remembered, from when he was at the beach, which part he felt would be the best to stop the tractor-trailer and unload - the real problem was how quickly it could be done. He was fatigued, and remembered the saying he heard his veteran Grandfather say, "Fatigue makes cowards of us all," which he wasn't sure his Grandfather came up with or if they were the words of another. It rang true, at least.

He parked the tractor-trailer around the area he studied earlier. Cautiously, he stepped outside the vehicle and skipped briskly around the block, looking around for late-night beach goers, police officers and general wanderers.

Crime takes place at night, he imagined. The point he chose to make the sprint from the back end of the tractor-trailer to the edge of the Pacific was the shortest in distance from any other point, and he needed the accessibility. He thought about driving the tractor-trailer over the small rock barriers, through the sand and steering the back end of the tractor-trailer so that it faced the water and he could chuck the fish out, but he worried about getting the tractor-trailer stuck in the sand and potentially horrendous problems associated with that.

With the coast clear, he opened the rear-end of the vehicle, crawled in, grabbed a carton of fish and dropped it outside - then another, then another. He did it until the pavement outside the door had cartons stacked on top of each other and he wanted to take a run. He then, carton by carton, picked them up and ran the X number of feet (not measured) to the edge of the ocean - it was difficult for him to tell the exact distance - and dumped the frozen fish into the ocean. He wasted no time taking one carton and running back to the tractor-trailer and picking up another carton. Over and over he did this, in a mad frenzy, while keeping an eye all around him. He wasn't clever enough for an alibi.

As he was bringing carton after carton of fish, and piling the fish in the same spot along the edge of the end of the tide, a large pile was forming that did not budge. He had stupidly thought the tide would flush them back into the water, but it did not, and they just laid there, one eye to the darkened heavens. By the time the payload was barren and the last runs were being made, he had an added issue to deal with: removing the sight of the clumps of fish. He ran the last carton to the tractor-trailer, threw all of the empties inside, closed the back as quietly as he could and made one last run back to the ocean. Using his hands and his soaked sneakers, he pushed and kicked the fish farther and farther out, deeper and deeper, until the pile had been leveled and it was just one thick layer of fish on the sand. He kept kicking and kicking, splashing too, until the fish were submerged and mostly out of sight. And as he proceeded further out, to ensure their absorption by the sea, in so far that he was waist-deep in water, he felt a strange tingling sensation around his legs and waist, and bubbles formed in a violent, living circle around him, hot, feverish and uncontrollable. He felt scared by the feeling of the warm cauldron, and frantically high-stepped his way out of the water, head and body tingling and frenzied. He saw some stragglers lying on the beach that never went into the water, but he didn't care - they'd join the others eventually, or never. When he did get out of the water, onto the sand, he sat facing away from the water and shook. He turned and stared hard into what he could see of the Pacific, foaming and churning, now with new additions.

Feeling chilled and barely able to walk in a straight line, he managed to get into the tractor-trailer and drive away, his numb feet and legs applying just enough pressure to depress the pedals. The tractor-trailer finally had a light payload. He looked upwards to the sky, and noticed that but a sliver of the moon was visible, which worked to his advantage, since a full moon would have made him and the tractor-trailer that much brighter.

25.

Amelia and Cameron awoke around 10 o'clock in the morning and peered over to the other bed to see if Marcel was in it - he was, half on top, half under the covers, still wearing the same clothes from the previous day. They figured they'd let him rest while they went for breakfast. Cameron walked outside after changing his t-shirt, brushing his teeth, putting on deodorant; Amelia was busy writing a note for Marcel - *Went out to eat be back later* - and then went to the bathroom with some supplies and shut the door. Cameron stretched out in the parking lot and walked over and took a look at the tractor-trailer that was parked cockeyed against the back fence.

They went to the local diner that specialized in strawberry waffles but instead bought biscuits and gravy and orange pekoe tea. Neither of them could be considered morning people, so the conversation was non-existent - Cameron's eyes flittered from the cup of tea to the window exposing the slowly emerging 74° day and Amelia's head leaned against his shoulder - they were sitting right next to each other - and she was somewhere between alert and asleep. Inside of the cup of tea, which was exceptionally hot, Cameron stared at the swirls of steam and spitting bubbles after it had been stirred: it was like Godard's Coffee Mug, and within the steaming black, the universe. It was an elegant shot in a master visualist and staunch contrarian's career, he thought to himself - too bad there was a massive drop-off in quality after the 70's. The counterculture dissipated, and things remained the same. So close, yet so far away, JLG. So far away.

They both thought and sat and eventually opened their mouths to discuss their plans on how they were going to relax for the day - to do what Marcel did the day before? To slog across the beach? Take in the ocean? They talked to the waitress for her advice, and she gave them details on the 'nicest beach around,' that was easy to get to and was rarely crowded. Directions were drawn up on a napkin.

They paid for their breakfast and returned to the hotel, and Marcel was first waking up. He thanked them for the note and asked about plans. They told him what the waitress said and he nodded and yawned. Marcel expressed disapproval in any potential plan to go to the San Diego Zoo, and Amelia and Cameron weren't in the mood to go anyway. None were in the mood for crowds and lines.

Cameron drove them to the beach at the Hotel del Coronado, over a snake-like elevated bridge. The waitress said that each time she'd gone there, she was usually one of only a few people there, and she liked to sit and read - the Hotel folk didn't bother you, and it was inordinately clean. They tipped the waitress well for her helpfulness and made sure, on the way out, to buy an extra muffin for Marcel, who ate it on the drive.

Having set up their territory with blankets, hotel towels and some packaged sweets and fruits, Cameron and Amelia dashed to the ocean with their plain old shirts and shorts on - they were too lazy to dig through the bags in the back of the tractor-trailer to check where their actual bathing suits were. Before they ran off, Amelia gave Marcel her cell phone and demanded he call home. Marcel made some excuse not to, but she insisted, and he gave in.

On the second ring, Lucile's voice could be heard.

LUCILE: Hello?

MARCEL: …

LUCILE: (*Pause*) Dave? Is that you?

MARCEL: Who's Dave?

LUCILE: (*Exhales*) Oh, it's you. Where are you calling from?

MARCEL: (*Repeating*) Who's Dave?

LUCILE: Someone I know. What did you do that for?

MARCEL: You mean leave?

LUCILE: Leave *like that* and not say anything? You snuck out.

MARCEL: That's why I'm calling. To explain myself.

LUCILE: You don't have to explain yourself.

MARCEL: (*Pause*) Look, I'm on a beach in San Diego. I have time to - wait, do you have time to talk? Or are you seriously waiting for a call?

LUCILE: No.

MARCEL: Okay then.

LUCILE: If you're worried, everything is taken care of.

MARCEL: What do you mean by that?

LUCILE: All of us panicked when you disappeared, so we started calling around. We went through your room looking for phone numbers but couldn't find any. We tried some old numbers for Cameron and Amelia but they didn't work. A few days later, Josef actually called here and told me everything that happened, and then Dad talked to Josef.

MARCEL: What - why did Josef call you?

LUCILE: I don't know. To talk.

MARCEL: He called you from school.

LUCILE: Yes, why?

MARCEL: (*Pause*) I don't understand why he would call you at home.

LUCILE: He always calls. Why?

MARCEL: Well, what did he tell you?

LUCILE: He said something about helping everyone move. Mom and Dad were pissed, but they talked to Josef a long time and somehow he took care of things. You owe him.

MARCEL: No one's mad at me?

LUCILE: They were mad, now they're just worried.

MARCEL: Tell them I'll pay back everything I owe if need be.

LUCILE: Are you coming home?

MARCEL: I want to drop Amelia and Cameron off. I'll stay for a bit.

LUCILE: I would try to come home sooner.

MARCEL: So... how's your Summer of Excess been, otherwise?

LUCILE: You're changing the subject.

MARCEL: (*Louder*) I don't want you telling anyone I called you.

LUCILE: What do you want me to say?

MARCEL: Say you talked to me some other time. Late at night.

LUCILE: What difference would that make?

MARCEL: Please do as I ask.

LUCILE: Okay. (*Pause*) Did you see anything interesting?

MARCEL: Some things. I'll tell you about them later.

LUCILE: You could send postcards.

MARCEL: All right, I have to go.

LUCILE: Go then.

MARCEL: I will.

LUCILE: Bye.

MARCEL: Bye.

The conversation ended.

After a long day at the beach, they left and returned to downtown San Diego. To conserve money, they ate sandwiches with potato chips at a low-cost deli. Foolishly, none of them allotted themselves a set amount of money to spend per destination point, but Junior Economist Cameron eased fears and killed the point by making some statement to the extent of money being irrelevant since God did not grow it and assign the need for man to spend it - it was a mechanized creation of man, a foolish evil humanity unleashed upon itself. That said, the sandwiches cost less than $20, or a green piece of printed-paper assigned the value of twenty one-dollar bills.

Amelia, having read from Twain how cold and unpleasant San Francisco summers were, wanted to go shopping in Neiman-Marcus for a sweatshirt so she had one when she got there. Cameron and Marcel didn't feel like doing any sort of shopping, so instead they went to one of the countless bars in the area and told her to meet them there when she was finished. At the bar they chose - purely at random - there was outdoor seating so they could gawk at the people in flux. Cameron took the opportunity to speak:

THE MOVIE STORE AROUND THE CORNER

CAMERON: I didn't tell Amelia this because she wouldn't approve, and I'm not sure she should, but I figured you'd like to hear it. It isn't too long.

At the video store I worked at, there was a high, high turn-over rate - people didn't want to stay, they found better jobs, they moved out of town. I didn't find it to be difficult, and wasn't in a feverish hurry to get out, though I was placing resumes actively for other places. I didn't want to get too-too lazy and stagnate. Because I stuck around, I remained one of their only reliable employees or at least that's what they told me. I usually worked days, but once in a while I had to do the night shift. It wasn't often.

The people that came in and out were from all walks of life, and all had some explanation as to how they got there. I listened, of course, since I had nothing better to do, and was always amazed at how people were capable of opening up to absolute strangers. They'd be telling me about their wives or kids - and this was while they were getting the newest release or rummaging in their wallets for their membership card. One guy came in every two days and took out some three or four films each time - I never asked him why so many, or how he found the time, but there he was, one day, explaining to me how he was out on work release and hurt his back and came from a Calvinist family who forbade movie watching and that he needed to catch up.

The one woman that was hired to work days with me was Melanie, who was on the short side and had hair like Elizabeth Taylor. She was quiet at first and slow in figuring out the computer - doing credits and exchanges tripped me up too - but I showed her and if she ever called over to me while I was stocking shelves I usually dropped everything to help her.

During slow days - Mondays and Tuesdays were always bad because that's when the new releases came in and needed to be labeled, put in the computer and shelved alphabetically - we talked about this or that, how she got laid off from the previous job she had - something secretarial - and how she needed to keep her nights free so she could take courses to become a Dental Hygienist. She was still young and still had plans, but evasive and vague whenever I tried to go farther with the conversation. I just listened to what I didn't understand, and let it go at that.

One particular day she came in and told me she was dropped off by a friend and that she needed a ride back home, and would I take her. I figured it wouldn't be a big inconvenience and that I had nothing else to do, so why not? She thanked me numerous times and I told her not to mention it, it was all right. After work, on the way to her home, I asked her what happened, and she said that her car was in the shop and needed some new part she never heard of and it was going to be a while.

This happened for several days. I kept asking what was going on with the car and she huffed, saying that 'the part' was on backorder and that if I didn't want to keep taking her home she'd work out other arrangements. I said it was okay, I didn't mind, I was just curious. She seemed to be opening up to me, and I was very grateful.

At the end of a Thursday, when I pulled the car in front of her home, she invited me inside and I turned off the car and followed her in. I'd be lying if I said I wasn't attracted to her, and wasn't waiting for her to ask. I kissed her in the hallway the moment the door shut behind us, and the two of us tangoed up the steps - not Astaire and Rogers, it was more like the Fumbling Duo, but we made it after I stepped on her feet a couple of times. She was passionate and patient, and a true comfort to be near. I did my best to seem brash and confident, and may not have been successful, but I think she understood. I didn't know at 8:00 AM that we would be together at 5:30 PM.

What first struck me as being peculiar was how she rushed me out of bed. I asked her what was going on, and she told me she forgot, she needed another ride, that we needed to hurry, so I should get dressed. I did rush, and while rushing I asked several questions, like "Where?" and "Why?" but she was quickly brushing her teeth and washing her face.

We got in the car and I asked her if we were in a hurry. "No hurry," she said, "but I said I'd be there by now." We drove about fifteen minutes until we got to a row of apartment buildings and she told me to keep the engine running. She went up to the one house, rang the bell, the door opened, a woman answered and the two of them went inside. Within minutes, Melanie came back out with a baby in her hands and a tote bag across her arm. I opened the door for her and she got in with the baby. She said, "It's too bad the Baby's car seat is in my car. Now I have to hold him." Before driving off, I turned to look at the woman in the doorway who was waving to her. Melanie waved back. She told me to go slow.

What I could piece together from the little she told me on the drive back was that the child was hers, that she got pregnant while she was taking classes, was forced to quit school by her parents and get a full time job, that she was tempted to get rid of the child but did not and was now being helped by her Aunt who volunteered to take care of the baby during the weekends since she was a medical writer who worked out of her own home. She was trying to start over again, and her Aunt offered to help in any way she could.

The fact that she had the baby made me feel guilty and upset, but what finalized it was when she told me at work the next day that her husband, who was in the Army and stationed in Seoul, had sent her a package with photographs of him and some of his fellow soldiers and a ratty scarf that he bought for her which she loved. "You're married?" I exclaimed, and became tense. She looked at me like I was overreacting and made some comment about the ring on her finger that I did not notice but was very obvious. I was ... very angry with myself. She told me not to worry about it, that it was nice, that it was a moment. "No big deal," she told me. Her husband had been gone for a year and a half, and she loved him deeply, and it was he who bought her and their child the house before he left.

After that, I barely spoke to her. She needed another ride, much later on, which I begrudgingly gave, and went straight home. She gave her notice a few months later when she said she found a better-paying job doing some typing work that her Aunt - once again - helped her find, and it was closer to her home. But I never knew how to treat her. I wished her good luck and best wishes, but I was tentative in saying it. She realized I wasn't acting the same and we only exchanged words when necessary. After the fact, I realized it was better when I knew nothing about her.

26.

All three spoke well of San Diego after leaving with the tractor-trailer - they returned the rental car before checking out of the hotel. Their final leg of the trip was ahead, and all three lamented how they wanted to spend more time at such-and-such place and spend the weekend high-and-low; they could have taken diversions here-and-there and explored this-and-that. They could, they assumed themselves, later on - they were still young. They could do anything they wanted.

They took Interstate 5, which broke off to US-101 all the way north - they passed horizontal, pitiless Los Angeles, which Cameron wanted to drive through one day, as well as Santa Barbara, but all were mostly interested in the periodic glimpses of the Pacific to their left. While emotionally back in a land of youth and comfort, Amelia talked about visiting her Grandfather in the nursing home in Southeastern New Jersey, in a town close to Atlantic City, and spending the day with her Mother:

THE NURSING HOME

AMELIA: My Dad didn't want to go with my Mom to visit with us. Dad told me it was okay if I didn't want to go either, but I wanted to see this nursing home my Grandfather was staying in myself. I didn't have plans with friends and thought to make a day of it - or at least a few hours. I also didn't know my Grandfather very well, which probably had something to do with my going.

My Grandfather, I gathered, after hearing all the stories that came out over the next couple of years and piecing them together, was a dominating and bitterly unpleasant man who, after open heart surgery, breathed better and felt better, but his mind went on him, his dementia became worse and since he was no longer able to take care of himself in his home - my Grandmother and he got divorced twenty years prior - he had to be put in a home. My Mom worked out the details, sold his small two-bedroom house and helped pick out the right nursing facility. He lived about an hour away from our house outside of Philly, but Dad insisted we keep him "out there," because he didn't want to have anything to do with the man.

My Dad's hostility was understandable, and it's clear why: my Mother's Father was a bear to my Mother, and to my Mother's Mother, who gambled away their savings, cheated on my Grandmother with her Sister and, from what I gather, was always a "womanizer." At 70, he flew to Hawaii by himself to "celebrate" with young Hawaiian girls, whom he had taken pictures with. It was these photos that he had obnoxiously pasted on the living room walls of his home, and not a single one of any member of his family.

When my Mom and I saw him, he was frighteningly thin and barely coherent - Mom and I sat across from him and listened, but nothing was clear. We were there to keep him company, and to pay respects. Mom, I felt, was doing it out of obligation.

A month earlier, Mom received a call from the nursing facility saying there was a problem with my Grandfather and they needed to set up a meeting to discuss it with her. It seems my Grandfather was found ... now, keep in mind these patients all lived on the same floor, in a barely-sterile atmosphere ... they found him and what they termed a "lady friend" in bed together. Mom avoided graphic detail with me around, but she said that he and this "lady friend" were originally seen holding hands and walking around the floor together during the day - while this was not considered negative behavior, it made the nursing staff notice and pay close attention. They told Mom that they had to intervene to separate the two at night, and that my Grandfather "became violent" - he always had a cane with him - and needed to be restrained. It happened once after that, they told her, the following day, and that was when they needed to send him to another center for treatment. She asked why they couldn't treat him, and they said it was because they didn't have the proper "tools," whatever that meant.

The day we visited was the day after he came back from his treatment. Mom tried to ask him what happened or what was wrong, but Grandfather wasn't able to tell either of us - he either shrugged or yawned - and when Mom pressed, he waived his hand at her and dismissed her questioning. Mom tried to get detailed information from the nurses on the floor, but they were pretty vague, saying they were required by the state to inform the patient's offspring of any procedures taken with the patient, and that they didn't have any more information than what she was already provided.

The three of us took a walk around the sidewalks of the building - it was encouraged by the staff at the facility to take them outside when you visited. The air was cool but not cold, and my Grandfather was wearing his pajamas and refused to change, so Mom put his coat and knit cap on him and we walked him downstairs.

Across the street from the nursing facility sat an elementary school and a large field that was part baseball diamond and part open land. The school only took up a small piece of the large area, and he wanted to go over there. We all walked over, very slowly - especially slow because they took away his cane and did not permit him to use a walker - and he stopped at one point in the grass and just stood there. While pointing, he got choked up and told us that he went to school there when he was a boy, and how he had a good friend he grew up with who went into the Marines with him and started relaying the stories of the people he was stationed with overseas, and Mom had to nudge him to move because we had to go back.

After we said goodbye and motioned to the nurses we were leaving he went back with the others on the floor to watching television and eating ice cream in a cup. I told my Mom that his story about this boy he grew up with and fought in The War with that died was sad, and asked if she ever heard it before. She said she did, but that it "wasn't true." "He was born and raised in Brooklyn," she said, "and wasn't drafted because he had scoliosis. I don't know where he heard that from, but it didn't happen. *That's* sad."

My Grandfather died five months later of malnutrition as a result of the disease.

27.

The Troupe arrived in San Francisco at night, and unfortunately for them, an unearthly darkness was covering the entire area - it was so bad that the police had to use road flares and direct traffic themselves with high-powered flashlights. Amelia called Naomi on her cell phone to get some kind of direction, and in order to find out what street they were at, Cameron had to yell out the side window and down to fellow drivers and pedestrians and police officers to find out where they were. What should have taken - at most - twenty minutes to get to took closer to an hour and a half.

Marcel's Custom Travel Booklet was finally rendered useless now that he found his destination, but was proud of by how far it got him. After he parked the tractor-trailer outside Naomi's home/complex, and while Cameron and Amelia were picking their frozen bags of luggage and personals out of the nooks of the back of the tractor-trailer - they were jostled around a lot - he made sure to keep the Booklet in a safe place and not throw it away by placing it in the glove compartment and locking it.

He went over to meet Naomi, slender and gracious, who was helping with Cameron and Amelia's things and brandishing her own flashlight. Marcel remarked how crippling the darkness was to traffic and she agreed, but energy would be restored eventually. "You make do," she said. Before they walked into her home, he tried to catch a glimpse of its location and size, but it was no use - he was also worried about the tractor-trailer sitting in the street, to which Naomi told him, "People will get around it."

The inside was neither lavish nor cluttered - it was, however, professionally done and designed, with classical reproductions on the walls and some abstract statues spread throughout - Naomi told them that a friend of her Mother's was a well-known interior decorator who even did celebrity homes in Beverly Hills and she worked on Naomi's house/complex for free. Naomi showed them the different rooms and the three floors - it was so spacious and so empty that it made sense to Marcel why she would invite friends to live with her. It wasn't like New York City where four people shared a flat because of economic necessity; it was like there was so much space she wanted to fill it with other people. This was, of course, Marcel's first impression.

Since they didn't eat yet, she had pizza in the kitchen on the first floor waiting for them - it was lukewarm but no one bothered to heat it up. After eating, she took them to their rooms, which were on the second floor. On that floor, there was a combined total of six available rooms and two bathrooms - one for men and one for women. The rooms were divided into two groups as well: three doors had the word "Male" engraved on them and three had "Female." Naomi laughed about the setup with them, and said that they could pick whichever room suited them - Marcel wanted the one closest to the bathroom, which Cameron wanted, but Cameron, for the umpteenth time, just gave in.

The rooms were furnished with matching furniture and basic components: a closet, a television and a bed. There was a dresser for clothes and a miniature refrigerator for personal food items. The three of them spent the rest of the night getting their rooms ready and relaxing and would talk extensively in the morning. When he saw her, Marcel thanked Naomi for making the sacrifice, but she said it was a delight.

The next day they ate breakfast down in the kitchen while watching the news broadcast playing on the kitchen monitor with the sound off and the Closed Captioning on - the power had been restored to the place much earlier. Naomi was telling Amelia and Cameron about some of the local theater companies they were going to visit and about some people she wanted them to meet - regarding their real jobs, Naomi had a few places in mind for them. All was tentative and unrushed - generating a friendly acquaintance with the city and its strangers was a good first step.

Marcel tagged along with them wearing a baseball hat he borrowed from Cameron and with a coat on. He was included in conversations with some of the new people they met up with, but something felt wrong to him - maybe it was discomfort with new conditions, maybe it was the fact that he had no place left to go, that the East Coast to West Coast Action of theirs was over. He looked in some of the shops to see what they offered, and studied a "Now Hiring" sign in the window of a clothing store very closely. He mostly listened to Naomi tell them about some of the nicest places in town, some small anecdotes and stories about friends she was impressed with. Marcel inhaled.

Six days after their arrival, Cameron had a dream that he awoke from, shot straight out of bed in a panic, heart racing. He looked at the clock: it was 3:42. He didn't lie back down to return to sleep immediately; he sat up and tried to regain his breath:

THE DREAM OF THE LOCUSTS

CAMERON: I was in an enormous field with dark, burnt patches of dry grass. Above me was a blanket of locusts or hornets making the most horrible sound, like a thousand voices yelling at once. I couldn't turn around to get a good look at them - I was face down in the dark, smoldering grass, crawling with my hands and knees. I remember trying to get up at one point - I had to stand - and the forces of the insects caused me to fall back down and frantically swat them away from the back of my head and my neck and my ears. Although I didn't know it at first, I was not alone in the field - there were men and women and children, all lying there next to me. To my left was an old man who looked straight through me. I asked him why we were crawling around on all fours and why the bugs wouldn't stop and go away. The old man said the reason I couldn't stand was because man's spine hadn't developed enough to stand, that man stood too much when he was supposed to crawl, like the oversized bee with tiny wings that wasn't designed to fly but did. The man was still talking when I awoke.

28.

For the next four - or was it more? - months, Amelia, Cameron and Marcel all landed new jobs - part-time, so they could focus on their side-projects and genuine interests. Amelia was hired at the same clothing store Marcel noticed his first full day in town while Cameron went for another gig at a movie rental store (he told Marcel it was all because he didn't feel like "learning a new trade") and Marcel worked at a coffee and cigar bar, which Naomi personally arranged for him because she knew the Manager who she said she went to school with, though what school Marcel never discovered.

Amelia and Cameron joined some local groups and wiggled their way into a few original plays, which Marcel contented himself watching from conception to finished product delivered to the paying public. He told both of them that he thought they should try to do some "established works" by "established writers" and that they were - and he put this gently - wasting their time with hackneyed amateur productions that were part comedy sketch and part political criticism, but with only youthful giddy energy and rampant silliness: the plays were an embarrassment to the performers, because they weren't funny to anyone other than those who wrote it. The once-attempted "serious" play Cameron had a small bit in was a valiant attempt to shed light on teenage pregnancy and romantic failure in high school, but ended on a ridiculous scene wherein the lead teenage girl - intended to be from the South, because the actress sported a horrendously fake drawl - and her forty-year-old lover sat on the stage and played a few random notes on a xylophone that appeared out of nowhere - "a dream sequence," was the author's notation in the text. Pinter it was not - although Nunnally Johnson would argue Pinter was simply fragmented tomfoolery assembled by the intellectual elite - and when out in the street he gathered that the others in the audience felt the same way he did: fretfully disappointed.

Neither Amelia nor Cameron paid any attention to Marcel's admittedly earnest attempts at advice, but since they hadn't asked him for it in the first place, his offering it was seen as an affront. They were not mad at him, exactly, but they tuned his comments out - and he, though wanting to go elsewhere to do something else, just kept coming to their rehearsals and meetings out of pure habit. The other actors and actresses didn't mind his presence, mainly since he never dared say anything to them and because they felt - or at least some felt - that he was just another audience member.

One young woman that was active in the underground, Françoise, actually went into the audience during their practice performance - she was in a play with both Amelia and Cameron - and walked right over to Marcel, who was sitting quietly and studying, to ask him about what he thought about a situation they couldn't resolve and needed input on. He'd never been asked by anyone, ever, what he thought, so he hadn't collected his ideas and comments yet and couldn't give a definite answer. He, on impulse, implored them to try a couple of things again, but felt he needed - nay, demanded - time to think it over.

Françoise, for the times they rehearsed afterwards would, when she had a break or no lines, come over and sat by Marcel and watch the stage from his vantage point. She was forward but endearing, and not as headstrong as Marcel had feared she would be during their first meeting. After rehearsal, Marcel invited her to stop by the coffee and cigar bar for some free cappuccino and the two of them could talk and relax. She agreed, and they spent the late evening hours together. He told her about the Action that was taken from the Atlantic to the Pacific, and she talked about friends in Chicago she wanted to see - and she recanted the famous statement: if you want to be in movies, go to Hollywood; if you want to be an actor, go to Chicago. When they didn't talk about the theater, they discussed her childhood in Winnipeg, her dropping out of college and the year she spent in Dublin "doing absolutely nothing."

Marcel had also kept in touch with Lucile while away, keeping regular contact by telephone. He missed her and he missed his family, in a way, but he wasn't sure if he was ready to go back. He contemplated taking buoyant and wispy Françoise - who Cameron referred to, more than once, as "Gene Tierney's double" - along with him on his way back and dropping her off in Chi-town, but was undecided. He talked to Naomi and Amelia one night:

AMELIA: What do you feel you need to do?

MARCEL: I don't know. It's nice here, and all, but....

NAOMI: You can go and come back. (*Smiling*) Your room will be guarded with fervor.

MARCEL: I think I have to go.

NAOMI: I hope you don't think we're pushing you out.

MARCEL: Absolutely not! I am grateful for everything.

Later that night, Marcel talked to Cameron about his plan, and Cameron told him he supported him in anything he wanted to do. He told Marcel that he should come and go as he pleased. Marcel noticed, while talking to Cameron that Cameron had painted on the door to his bedroom - beneath the "Male" - with black acrylic:

29.

In two weeks, Marcel and Françoise left San Francisco and headed northeast to Chicago. Françoise promised him a place to stay when they got there, but he said he'd decide what to do when he finally arrived, and the only thing he was sure of was that he had to return the tractor-trailer, which his Father had graciously and with formidable calm allowed him to hold on to, sooner than later. The tractor-trailer was his private, massive responsibility. Extra expenses and repairs for it were out of Marcel's pocket.

FRANÇOISE: It sounds like your Father is more understanding than mine.

MARCEL: A friend of mine and my Sister helped him achieve that understanding.

FRANÇOISE: (*Pause*) What made you ... do all this? What were you looking for?

MARCEL: I'm not sure. (*Pause*) I tend to wear things out. When I am in one place, I cannot wait to be in another. When I see what I want, I cannot stop thinking about getting it. Right now, I am with you. I am trying to change myself, but it's about taking small steps. Tiny, incremental movements forward.

FRANÇOISE: (*Smiles*) I'm glad to be with you.

MARCEL: Are you sad to be leaving San Francisco?

FRANÇOISE: (*Shrugs*) I'll return.

Marcel explained to Françoise the stories that were told on the way West, and if possible, she should add something of her own. She was already aware of this, curiously enough, and came prepared. She opened up her handbag and took out a Moleskine Notepad that was covered with stickers of all colors, and stuffed with folded papers and saved treasures. She pulled out several pieces from the back folding slot and read the following:

THE PATH OF SEXUAL MOMENTUM

FRANÇOISE: *The hypothalamus in the brain secretes gonatotropin releasing hormone into the blood vessels leading to the anterior pituitary gland. The anterior pituitary gland causes the anterior pituitary cells to release two hormones, luteinizing hormone and follicle stimulating hormone, into the general blood circulation. Luteinizing hormone and follicle stimulating hormone act on the testes/ovaries to stimulate the making and maturation of the sex cells and the production of three sex hormones: estrogen, testosterone, and progesterone (which serve to stimulate the growth of the sexual organs and secondary sexual features). The nerve cells time-release small, low-level spurts of gonatotropin releasing hormone every ninety minutes, which causes the anterior pituitary to secrete small pulses of luteinizing hormone and follicle stimulating hormone. The sex hormones from the testes or ovaries give feedback to the hypothalamus and anterior pituitary to regulate the secretion of gonatotropin releasing hormone, luteinizing hormone and follicle stimulating hormone - this interplay is the 'negative feedback control system.'*

Numerous types of stimuli - visual, mental, physical - can trigger sexual arousal. Nerve impulses from the brain cause heart rates to increase and dilate peripheral blood vessels. The Cowper's glands in the man and the vestibular glands in the woman secrete fluid that lubricates the man's urethra and the woman's labial area and vagina. The man's brain sends nerve impulses to the blood vessels in his penis and tells the arterioles to dilate and the venules to constrict. The blood flow engorges the spongy tissue of his penis, causing it to become erect.

Ejaculation occurs when muscle contractions in the epididymis, prostate and seminal vesicles propel semen from the penis into the woman's vagina at the base of the uterine cervix. The exact path is as follows: seminiferous tubule to epididymis to vas deferens to seminal vesicle (sugar, amino acids and vitamin C) to prostate gland (alkaline fluid to neutralize acids in female) to bulbourethral gland (more alkaline fluid and lubricant) to urethra and finally out of the male. Muscle contractions in the woman's body periodically dip her cervix into the semen to aid the sperm cells through the reproductive tract.

Sperm begin a long journey to fertilization: they must first cross the barrier of the cervix. Once the sperm have traversed the cervical mucus, they travel up the moistened lining of the uterus into the Fallopian tubes. Only one of the Fallopian tubes contains an egg, so many sperm travel in the wrong direction. Few actually reach the Fallopian tubes.

www.ingramcontent.com/pod-product-compliance
Lightning Source LLC
Chambersburg PA
CBHW021235130626
46554CB00004B/1506